Providence Trail

I0553623

By
Kenneth M. Lee

Providence Trail
By Kenneth M. Lee
Copyright ©2025
ISBN 9780971185098

Printed in the United States of America

This is a work of fiction, though the U.S. Civil War did occur, and the towns mentioned, are real. Otherwise, names, characters, and incidences are purely the works of imagination. Any resemblance to actual persons, living or dead, businesses, offices, or companies, are purely coincidental.

Kenneth M. Lee
1382 Grandpa Ln.
Loris SC 29569

E-Mail: <u>kenlwor@gmail.com</u>

Books by Kenneth M. Lee

Persecuted But Not Forsaken

Devotional Books

God's Help Now! (Out of Print)
Devotions A-Z
God's Divine Help
Southern Devotions

Devotional Booklets

Quiet Heavens, 4 Editions (Out of Print)

Fiction Books

The Marcia Lane Suspense Series (3)
Victim's Vengeance
Unveiled
Jewel Time

All books are available for order at Amazon.com (U.S.) marketplace on the Internet.

1.

I was sitting against an oak tree on a hill looking down into Petersburg wondering where a contingent of Yankee soldiers was going on this cool day in 1865.

The gnats were not too bad, but the ants were beginning to move on the dirt beside me, searching for food, and getting close to my legs.

I swished them away with a gathering of pine straw and watched where I put my hands down on the ground to steady myself.

I was a scout for the Confederate Army – and it was a lot better than being on the front line of battle and being shot at, which was happening below.

But I was always alone, except for when I delivered messages to Generals at camps, or made connections with another scout or spy.

Sometimes I had to walk behind Yankee lines to see what I needed to see – and then find my way to the closest Confederate camp.

I didn't have anyone telling me what to do, until I got to one of the camps, and even then, I was left to make decisions on how to accomplish a mission.

I chewed on a birch twig and looked out over the horizon, through an assortment of maple and oak trees, to see any other evidence of blue shirts.

There were about 1,000 smart looking Yankee soldiers marching along a road from the north, with another contingent of a hundred men behind them, on horses, which were pulling wagons and cannons; the horses walked slowly to avoid ruts and mud puddles. Some men in officer uniforms were on each side of the marching soldiers.

They had to be reinforcements, I thought. And then it dawned on me, the Yanks were going in the direction of the railroads.

Five trains and a host of wagon trails intersected at Petersburg, with many of them going to Richmond, the capital of the Confederacy.

I put my field glasses down and watched some of the ants climb up the bark on the high side of the tree.

I hoped the twig that I had snapped off along a river and spit out nearby would not be a target for them: such things had happened before.

I liked sweet birch, and I hoped it would sweeten me up in case I got to a friendly town and met a woman.

But with the rags I was wearing, after months of being in fields of rain, snow, and mud, I'd be lucky to be allowed in town -- much less find a place to eat and be with a woman.

I brushed away a bed of winter's leaves and stretched out. The sun was shining through the trees, so I moved to get into some shade. There was no need to be an easy target for the Yankees.

I was wondering what I could eat for dinner: I was tired of groundnuts and field corn.

I had seen what I needed to see. I looked for any forward Yankee scouts. Seeing none, I got up, brushed myself off, and looked for the safest way to walk to Richmond and tell General Lee what I had just seen.

I hurried down the hill following a deer trail to the bottom, and then I turned east, and hurried along a dirt road that I knew was safe and free of Yankees.

After a day's travel, I lay down for a couple hours near the James River and waited. I wanted to make sure the Yankees were not on the river in boats.

I found some pecans on the ground and ate them, crossed the river on a friendly raft, and went straight to Lee's Headquarters.

He welcomed me -- but had a disconcerting look on his face after I told him what was happening at Petersburg. No doubt he was concerned about the turn of events that had made Petersburg a target. General Beauregard and the troops were being slaughtered.

He thanked me for alerting him. He said to go back and tell the General that he would send reinforcements. "We have to keep those supply lines open," he said. "After that, find out what the Yankees are doing near Raleigh. General Johnston is on the west side near Garner fighting them."

I returned to the James River and ferried back to land. I walked to Petersburg and found General Beauregard.

I told him help was on the way, and that I had orders to head south. He thanked me and had a young boy go to the mess tent to get me some food.

It was well needed.

After I ate, I walked out of camp southward, but before I went too far, I had a plan to get another horse – after I had seen where those Yankees and their cannon loaders were heading.

My horse had turned up lame a week ago, so I had to shoot him, and I'd been walking ever since.

At some time, the Yankees would have to set up and camp. And since they'd be joyous with fresh troops and winning the war, I might be able to get a horse.

I didn't have to long to look. Firing started in the next morning, shortly after I had arose from a deep sleep under a bramble bush that wasn't a hundred yards away.

When the firing paused – and then started up again, I walked a spat and spotted a fine Morgan horse that was tied up to a tree behind the cannons.

Just before I heard the next volley of cannon balls, and the rhythmic sound of "fire" orders from the Yankee field officer, I jumped the horse.

With my knife, I cut the rope that was tied to him – I turned him around -- and with the wind being in my favor -- took off with cannon smoke covering my escape.

After weeks of meandering through the woods and finally reaching an area near Raleigh, I saw a battery of Yankees that was surely marching the wrong way. I didn't see any ambulances or wounded to warrant their backwards march: they were marching northward, which didn't make much sense.

I stopped and thought about it, and it finally dawned on me that the war may be over. The Yankees had us outnumbered, and had probably destroyed the supply lines.

When I got to the Confederate Camp, an officer asked where I'd been. I told him I was coming from Petersburg and I needed to talk with General Johnston.

The officer said Johnston was meeting with Yankee officers and surrendering at Durham. General Lee had surrendered his own forces a few days ago.

I wasn't surprised.

"There are a few rations left in the mess tent. Better get you some before they're gone," the officer said.

I saluted him, got off the horse, and grabbed the saddlebags that were attached to it. I tied the horse up to a nearby tree branch.

And then I went towards the mess tent.

Outside the tent, several men were lying on the ground resting and trying to recover from wounds. Two medics were changing a cloth bandage on one man's arm that had either been blown off or amputated.

I looked at the men with sadness and wished I could do something for them. But I figured the men would be going home as soon as they got the strength to walk or ride.

I couldn't worry about them too much -- I had my own problems -- having no money, home, or family.

I got a bowl of soup and sat beside a walnut tree thinking about things.

My foster parents' house I heard had been plundered, and they had left for parts unknown. I didn't have any money or decent clothes. I could always steal food from a smokehouse, corncrib, or root cellar. But where was I going to go?

After I finished the soup and gained a little strength, I moved the saddlebags over my lap and opened the leather cover of one side. I had looked earlier in this side but only seen a metal first aid kit.

I brought it out and released the two latches. The kit was full of surprises -- the Yankees having access to goods from the north that none of us Rebels had. There was a bar of soap, toothbrush, comb, razor, and some cotton cloth. I closed the kit and put it back.

Then I opened the cover of the other bag. There was a small dictionary and some wadded up paper at its bottom. I opened the dictionary carefully and flipped through the pages -- looking at words that I had never seen before. The officer had said to take a respite, and I was wondering where to get that.

I followed the r's in the dictionary and found that the word meant *relax*. I can do that, I thought.

I never had a dictionary. Only way I had learned to read was from words and stories in the Bible, which was the primary book at the home of my foster parents.

Relax. Good enough for me. I was about to put the dictionary back into the saddle bags when some pieces of paper fell out from its back cover -- Federal notes had been folded into quarter sections and tucked between the last few pages!

I grabbed them quickly, hid them inside my shirt, and hoped no one saw me. I looked around and there was not a soul looking at me; so I humbly took the bills and unfolded them: there was over $200 in federal notes!

I refolded them and tucked them safely into my pant's pocket. I hoped I wouldn't have to cross a creek any time soon; otherwise, I would need a skin bag.

Lastly, in a separate side pocket of the bag, was a folded one-page newspaper. The front of it said *The Hartford Tribune*. On the back of the paper were some ads, and one was seeking to employ a typesetter. I figured it had something to do with this newspaper, but when I looked further, a typesetter was needed for a paper in Kansas City.

I looked up the word typesetter and saw that it was a person who set type.

That was good enough for me. I stuck the paper back in its pouch and began to daydream: I'd love to write and print stories for a newspaper. Now that the war was ended, maybe it was time to fulfill the dream.

But I wondered if this horse could make it.

Right there, I named the horse Cinnamon, because he acted spicy at times with a quick head start and a jerk of his head.

I was filled up on all the soup I could muster. I washed the tin off in a nearby creek and took it back to the mess tent.

I put the bags back on Cinnamon, mounted him, and took off in the direction of a town I had marched through years earlier called AltaVista. I had taken a liking to it, and a woman, whose smile had permeated the street dust and met my eyes.

It took me a week to arrive at AltaVista, and she was still there. Grungy as I was, I walked up to her and wrapped my hands around her body in need of compassion.

Lucille cleaned me up, fed me, and nursed my wounds.

2.

I stayed in Lucille's pad for a couple weeks -- a little one-room shack at the end of town -- searching for my destiny. I was reading the newspaper, and I was reading a small Bible I kept with me.

My favorite verse in the Bible was Hebrews 6:12 – about not being slothful but followers of them who through faith and patience inherited promises.

I read this verse every night, while Lucille was shopping for petticoats, laced shoes, or being with another man.

I knew then where I was going: I wanted to be that typesetter, and according to this newspaper, one was needed in Kansas City.

Kansas was a good ways off, but what else did I have to do.

So one sunny morning, when the daffodils were spreading their yellow petals and forsythia bushes their yellow spikes, I packed my bags after an awful breakfast across the street at Freda's kitchen of guinea eggs and spoiled hog jowl, and I headed to the livery stable where Cinnamon was being kept by Charley.

When Lucille saw me walking down the road with my bags packed, she yelled at me from the upstairs window and said, "Be sure to take this!" And she threw a pair of my dirty socks out the window.

Charley was sitting on a fencepost smoking a magnolia leaf, or trying to, because there weren't any cigarettes at the store.

"Get Cinnamon ready Charley. I'm heading out for good."

"Where to Mr. Grange?"

"Well now, don't you tell a soul, but I'm going to Kansas for a job."

"Mighty long ways."

"I got to go Charley. There's nothing here for me, and from this newspaper I've been reading, the west is growing with economic opportunity. Lucille ain't making things any better throwing my clothes out the window."

"You got a point there. I see you still got your gun."

"And my cookware and wool cape. It's all I need."

Charley got off the fence, grabbed Cinnamon's bridle, and led him to the barn for feed.

It was a good day for starting a trip --the sky was clear and the wind was down on this May morning – a time when a man can start his destiny among spring's flooding steams and new plant growth.

There'd be plenty to eat along the way – everything from tree nuts to fresh greens in the pastures. I might be able to kill a squirrel, grouse, or deer too. But for a couple of days, I'd settle on making some time and chewing on corn pones and the salt pork that I had gotten from Freda's kitchen.

I walked back towards town and said goodbye to some friends. I came back to the livery stable a short while later to see Cinnamon fed and packed.

"You travel light over that mountain or Cinnamon will give out. These Morgans are strong but not built for rough terrain," he said.

"Will do Charley."

I mounted Cinnamon and checked that my saddlebags were girded and the rifle safely in the scabbard.

The boarding house across the street looked lonelier than ever, but it was early in the day, and hungry men wouldn't be looking for women -- until they got their bellies full of food and alcohol.

I wondered if Lucille felt any remorse about her falsely accusing me of getting fresh with other women, but there was no sign of her lifting up the curtains and peeking at me from the upstairs window. Probably she was already in bed with another man.

Who needs her, I thought. I'll eat and sleep in the woods. Besides, I need a job. There aren't enough people here to support a general store, much less a newspaper office, and that's what I want.

Cinnamon snorted a couple times and kicked up his heels as if to say, let's get going or get the pack off. It hurts a horse to stand still more than walk.

I got down off him and checked his rear legs just to make sure they weren't bitten or injured. Charley looked on with interest.

I climbed back up and felt the cool leather bridle straps in my hands. Charley had oiled the straps. I tossed Charlie one of the silver dollars that I had found in the saddlebags.

I turned the horse to the left and out of the stable area heading west.

3.

The sun was moving quickly above the horizon behind me when I took one last look at town, and it shone on the boarding house's white clapboard siding, as if it was to prick my conscience or something. It seemed like I couldn't get away from this segment of my life.

There was still no sign of a waving hand from Lucille.

I thought of an old saying: Absence makes the heart grow fonder. But the writer didn't know about the likes of Lucille.

I knew of a trading post at the foot of the Appalachian Mountains west of Asheville where I could get supplies before I crossed the mountain. It would take more than a few days to get there.

Each night, I lay down and wondered why Lee had not mobilized his forces at Gettysburg before the Yankees got there. When he did get there, the Yankees had high ground, and we were on the low. Anyone knows that a bullet or lead ball will go faster downhill than uphill simply by the weight of its makeup. But then Lee had a way of sending the Yankees one way, while his Calvary was tearing up rails, bridges, or roads in front of and behind them.

Reality must have struck him by the sheer numbers of Yankee soldiers, animals, and firearms at Gettysburg. And before he got there, many men had already lost their lives. He must have known surrender was inevitable.

I stopped occasionally to water Cinnamon and sat reading the dictionary.

The dictionary had many words I'd never seen in the Bible: they were called verbs, adverbs, interjections, conjunctions. And there were past and present endings for words. I mean I had to figure all this out if I was going to be a newspaperman and write stories for people to understand.

I figured it was the Yankee way of thinking and talking; they always liked to talk a lot from the few I had met.

This word difference became clearer when I read that articles, idioms, and interjections weren't used in the original Bible. I mean the Bible just gets to the point, didn't even have vowels for words in the original Hebrew text, kind of like the language in the South.

I mean if the sun is shining today in the south, the sun is shining. But from a Yankee's point of view, the sun is shining and it's getting hot and causing perspiration.

A Yankee will add a bunch more words that don't mean anything other than the sun is shining -- and in my mind, all the time thinking of a way to cheat you.

14

The Yankees, with unnecessary words, actually consider themselves to be smart for it, while a Southerner looks on in compassion at the waste of precious air and tongue waggling.

So this dictionary has made some difference in my thought process. I wasn't too worried about it, since Kansas was in the middle of the north and the south.

After a couple weeks on the trail, I reached Asheville and came to a fork in the road.

One way ventured off along a creek and the eastern side of the mountain, while the other began a long slow trek up the mountain and its peak at 6000 feet.

I knew from an engineer's map that I had seen earlier at a camp that I was staying along the creek until just past Asheville, and then I would go over the mountain.

There was a sign at the fork that showed a bed drawn on it, and I figured that would be a place to camp.

I went along the creek and came to the campsite: it had leftover charred wood on the ground from a fire that had been built.

I took to a large granite rock – that had names carved in it and scrape marks at the top-- where someone had sharpened a knife.

I tied Cinnamon to a limb just above the boulder.

Scrub brush and rhododendron trees were all around me. There were mostly firs and beech trees on the other side of the small creek. The trees dwarfed the area -- forbidding the sun's rays to hit the ground. The smell of mold and mildew lingered in the air, like being in a cave, where it's continually moist and there is no sun.

15

I took the bags from Cinnamon and laid them on the rock. I dropped my hat in the cool water of the creek and soaked my head with it.

I looked around for something to eat, and I saw some hickory trees. I found some wild onions and hickory nuts on the ground.

I laid the cape out next to the rock -- took Cinnamon to some green grass under a wild cherry tree and tied him up. I went back and lay down with my .44 caliber pistol tucked under my shirt and the Winchester rifle hid under the leaves beside me.

The sound of hoof beats awoke me some time later, and I awoke to see a heavily bearded man on a roan coming my way with the carcass of a deer on its back.

"Hey yoh, Mister," he said.

"Howdy Yo!" I said, with my pistol in my hand under my cloak. I gave him a friendly nod.

He looked as if he had been traveling for some time. The old man's face was weathered and wrinkled. Threads off his saddlebag waved with each step the horse took.

He looked me over, got down off his horse, and sat on a nearby boulder.

Must be a friendly chap or he was just plumb tired, I was thinking. But when men have been traveling for a while, there's a need to find another person and talk.

He took a wad of tobacco out of his front pocket and showed it to me.

"You want some?"

"No thanks. Just makes me hungry for food."

"I can understand that. That's why I chew! Where you headin' Mister?"

"Across the mountain, west."

"Oh no, no, no. You don't want to go there."

"Why not. A lot of people are – says there's gold and money to be made."

"Well, that's all fine if you don't get killed first."

"Well, who would do that?"

"Why, haven't you heard about the war? That's why I left."

"The war's over."

He looked at me like I was crazy.

"War ain't over in Missouri and Arkansas. Where did you hear that?"

"I was a scout for the Confederates, and General Lee surrendered to Grant in Virginia a few weeks ago."

"I'll be. That's news to me. Be nice if they surrendered out west. That where you're going?"

"Is."

We had a good talk about the weather and shared some coffee and pones; then he said he had to get on his way before the sun set and find a general store: his meat was surely to spoil if he didn't find some salt to preserve it.

After a little more napping, I got some energy and rode until the sun set -- right when the trail began to go slightly upward -- and it was getting colder.

4.

The general store was at the foot of the mountain near
Canton.

I stocked up with canned goods, a slab of cured bacon,
some rifle shells, and some saddle soap to soften the leather
straps and stop the chafing against my legs. I also bought a
woven blanket for the cold air over the mountain.

After I left the store, there were many twists and turns on
the trail, being as no trail goes straight up a mountain: it has
to be climbed slowly

When there was a sharp turn, the trail was usually worn
thin from water coming down its high side.

Cinnamon took his time when the trail narrowed, and it's
a good thing, because both of us would have gone over the
side and probably been killed from the fall.

But we made it to the top, and while I sat looking into the Tennessee Valley, I was wondering if I was doing the right thing.

But life isn't always about doing the right thing. I learned that during the war, where there wasn't a lot rules -- and when it came to staying alive.

And now, here I am, sitting a mile above sea level with no one in sight and nothing to depend but myself, Cinnamon, and two guns for protection.

Sitting quiet can bring good tidings. As Cinnamon and I were frozen in place, an eight point deer came in sight gnawing at berries on a bush.

I reached slowly to retrieve my Winchester, aimed at his head, and shot to knock him down. I wasn't in no mood to chase a wounded deer and look for bloodstains.

He dropped like a tree limb hit by lightning.

I got off Cinnamon and walked over to him. He had drawn his last breath, but to make sure and not kicked in the face, I moved him slightly with my gun.

Nothing. So I pulled him up and laid him down against a tree trunk. And I took my knife to his throat to bleed him out.

Then I gutted him, making sure not to cut the bladder. I scraped out the entrails. Flies and gnats saw my every move and began to swarm around the mess. The guts had to be buried, so I took a nearby stick and started digging at the ground, removing small rocks, and scraping hard dirt. It was ground I was not accustomed to, because many rocks were large and stuck. They weren't moving an inch, being quartz.

After moving one large stone, another would be underneath it. No wonder, it's a mountain, I thought.

I may as well have been trying to scrape metal off an iron post. I had never been on a hill this high.

So I looked for softer dirt, pried a knee-high boulder over with a hickory stick, and there it was.

I pushed the boulder away further and dug out a hole, slid the entrails into it, and covered them with dirt.

I knifed a leg and thigh off the deer and put the carcass on another boulder -- away from the blood stained ground area -- where the gnats wouldn't be so bad around the bloody stench.

I took my meat and went back to Cinnamon and my gear. I saw water seeping from a rock cavity, so I went over there and washed off the meat, my knife, and my hands.

I built a fire and roasted the deer over some rocks.

After I ate, I received some new energy. My doubtful thoughts disappeared, and I thanked God for His presence, the mountain, and the deer.

I then went back to get the rest of the deer. I washed off some dirt and leaves that were stuck to it.

Then I was worried about stray animals getting the deer.

Off to the side of the cliff were some tall trees that had grape vines running up their trunks and outward on the limbs.

I found one vine running along the ground, enough for hanging the deer from a tree limb so a bear wouldn't get it.

I cut the vine off and threw it up and over an ash tree limb -- about 15 feet up -- and tied its end to the deer's head and hoisted it.

The moon was beginning to set, and it cast a shadow on the deer hanging from the tree.

I stood there and watched the deer's carcass swinging from the hoisting and a gust of wind. I was satisfied in what I had done, and it was time to bed down.

But it was getting cold, and there wasn't a place to shelter myself from the wind other than boulders.

I went and got my leather cape, along with my blanket. I found a boulder that blocked the wind, and that's where I lay down.

That was about right as I could get, and I thanked God for that.

I sure wanted that deer fur to keep me warm, but it would have to wait.

5.

In the morning, I skinned the deer and laid its fur out for a couple hours to dry. I put all the meat in a burlap bag that I had brought with me.

It took me a couple days to get down the mountain. I had to hold Cinnamon back some rather than taking a tumble down steep slopes into rhododendron trees that were laced with fungus and mold from the winter's storms.

Stonecrop, trailing arbutus, and creasy greens were all along the trail.

I stopped at times and picked some of the greens. I ate some, and tucked some safely away in the saddlebags. The greens would be mighty fine cooked in deer's fat too.

Branch lettuce was also along the trails -- growing fervently on the tops of rocks along the banks of the creek. The lettuce was more abundant in sun-filtered areas.

There's nothing better than branch lettuce or crows feet greens fried in grease with corn bread. Maybe I would come across a cornfield. Then I could fry some corn kernels.

When I reached the bottom of the mountain, there were a few rolling hills to navigate and a couple of wide streams. Fortunately, the streams were rock and sandbar ridden, which made it easier for us to cross.

I stopped at a general store near Knoxville and re-stocked my supplies. I bought some can beans, dried meat, and hard tack biscuits, which needed only a little water to get them chewable.

Then I went towards Nashville.

Trails, which had been laced with mud prints from animals and wagons, now turned into hard packed dirt roads. The weather was very dry.

A few people were passing me – and they were heading west as I was. Several groups would be resting -- just off the road under trees or by creeks. They might be washing clothes, cooking, or working on their wagons.

I didn't stop to socialize much. I needed a job, and the war had brought out many conflicting emotions that people were dealing with, like loss of loved ones, property, and food stocks. Starting a conversation could last into the night.

There were outposts every so often where I could get a meal. Stage coaches were stopping at many of these outposts to deliver mail, let off passengers, or change horses.

It took me a couple of months and three river ferries to get to St. Louis, where I saw progress like never before.

There were wide docks along the Mississippi River, and steam powered boats on the river. On the roads, there were wagons that had metal bands around the wheels. People had on fancy clothes in town: high top hats, silk vests, and velvet petticoats.

I left St. Louis as soon I could and found a nice camping spot by the river where I caught some fish with a string and hook that I loaded with worms and crickets.

I stayed here for a couple days at the river trying to get my strength back and give Cinnamon a much needed rest.

In a private spot, I washed my clothes and let them dry on a bush on a sunny day. I re-oiled my gun, put some oil on my boots, and took the bar of soap from the saddlebag to my skin.

I saw a couple of Yankee ironclad boats travelling the river, but the men on them looked like civilians: they did not have blue uniforms on.

Several flat boats went by with logs on them.

Strangers said the war was still going on and to be very careful.

So I got off the main road and travelled alongside it the best I could, until I felt safe.

6.

I wanted to make a good impression at the newspaper office, if I ever got there and the job was still available. It had been months since the job was posted.

Cinnamon was in good shape, now feeding on winter stubble and green grass that was flourishing everywhere. And the roads were much better for him. I didn't push him -- walking about 20 miles a day was enough.

When I approached Kansas City, vultures were flying in circles over the town, and I figured that to be a garbage dump or a bone yard for dead cows. I had heard from a traveler that men were killing buffalo for hides and leaving their carcasses scattered all over the frontier.

The town's buildings looked similar to the ones at St. Louis: some were four stories tall and had stairs running down the sides.

And there were roads going in all different directions.

Tall trees bordered the southern perimeter along a curving creek. Single story wooden clapboard buildings lined the main road into town, and hitching posts were at several different places. There was a railroad track coming from the east, and there was a mercantile exchange and cattle pens near the railroad.

People were everywhere, crossing the main street, looking out from balconies, and riding on horses.

I was still wary of the Yankees, so I looked closely at each group of people. Sometimes, I wondered if I was just being paranoid, or maybe I had eaten too many wild mushrooms.

But no, I was being careful. It was going to take some time getting back to normal.

I had dressed Cinnamon up with a loomed shawl to hide his Morgan traits and keep the Yankees from identifying one of their horses.

I had also put a dried sheaf of tobacco on his hind parts, to make it look like I was in the trading business.

A corral was on the right of the road, and a wagon with a load of hay was just inside its gate.

Just as I passed it, I saw curtains move from a window in a nearby house, and hands that quickly took away from the window. The war had made everyone a bit cautious.

I made sure my Winchester slid easily in and out of its scabbard. There's nothing worse than to have to hurry and grab a rifle only for it to be stuck in the bottom of its holder. My pistol was in the saddlebags -- so it wouldn't rub across my side during the ride or get dirty.

I reined Cinnamon to a stop just past the house where the curtains closed. I stared and wondered about the hidden figure. If it was woman, I could be in luck.

A team of horses approached, so I nudged Cinnamon to the right trying to get away from the dust. The coach driver held the reins tightly trying to slow the animals down.

I looked at two of the visible passengers in the coach. They looked of fine degree with white ruffled collared shirts and black vests. One had a cigar pointed towards his mouth.

Once the dust settled, the curtains drew slowly back, showing a woman a woman of middle age with hair locks drooping over her ears and a loose fitting partially open brown shirt exposing the top of her chest.

My eyes took to it quickly, and I lost control of my mission.

She smiled at my motionless figure that was bent over leaning on the pommel.

There's something about a woman that can cause a man to freeze and lose thought of everything. But Lucille, being the last one, had only caused me to run away fast as I could.

I remembered an old saying about whatever a man puts into a woman is what he's going to get out.

But I never gave Lucille anything bad, and I wondered why things often didn't come out for good.

It was hard to figure.

7.

I nudged Cinnamon to the opposite side of the street to a small building that had a sign above it that said Wilma's Café.

I hitched him to a post in front of a window where I could watch him and my rifle, after I went inside.

I slapped my hat against my thigh and watched the dust fly off. There's nothing worse than entering a strange town and looking timid, because shysters are looking to take advantage of anyone that looks meek. But if it's one thing I learned as a scout, never be who you really are until you gauge the other person.

Feeling giddy for just making it here, and maybe being a newspaper man, I wanted to act like one. I put my hat back on and straightened my shirt collar.

I took my saddlebags and stepped onto the platform and opened the door.

There were four tables in the room and four chairs around each table. A cast iron stove was behind the counter at the rear.

A gray haired woman was flipping something on a stove from a pan that had smoke rising. From the smell of the room, it was bacon that was smoking. At this time, I could have eaten shoe leather.

She took a quick look at me and went back to her work.

There were two men sitting at a far table drinking coffee from tin cups and looking anything but like cow pokes.

One had on black britches and a yellow pressed shirt. The other man had on a brown suede shirt and khaki pants: his ivory colored leather boots on his crossed legs stuck out from the bottom of the table.

Both men were reading papers of some sort, and neither paid a bit of attention to me.

I put the saddle bags on an empty chair and drew another chair to sit on, thanking God all the time of finding such an accommodation, along with not getting shot at by any stray Yankee.

It didn't take long to find out it was Wilma doing the cooking when one of the men yelled her name for coffee.

She grabbed the pot, brought it over, and poured some in his cup; then she walked over to me.

"Good morning. Glad to have you here," she said.

"Glad to be here."

She took a rag from her apron and quickly wiped the table while asking me where I was from.

Her gray dress became her tired face, which was wrinkled, yet she was adept in her talk. Her words were clear and smooth. A red checkered apron with a pocket was tied around the front of her dress, and she put the rag back in it.

I didn't tell her where I was from -- just said I was passing through and might stay if I liked it.

"Well. There ain't a whole lot here right now but this is place is growing. The railroad finished laying a spur and this is the gateway to the west."

"Sounds like it's ripe for growth," I said as I took my scarf from around my neck and began to relax.

"It is. People got to have a place to trade their goods to the east. That would be good for you if want a job."

I nodded my head.

"I would ask what you'd like but we only cook what we got," she said with a wry smile. "Biscuits and gravy, grits, and sliced jowl."

"That sounds good. Got any eggs?"

"Sure."

"That will do with coffee."

"Be right back."

Wilma turned and went to the stove area. She reached down on the floor and moved something, and I hoped it wasn't a rat.

She reached to a counter, got a chunk of a side meat, and sliced off a few pieces.

She threw them on the grill, and the smoke reached high into the air. She reached into a container and took out a couple of biscuits and put them next to the smoking jowl.

After a couple minutes, she cracked two eggs and put them in the pork's hot grease on the griddle.

8.

Outside the window, the sun was a quarter way up and people were walking on the wood planks that lined the streets. Without the planks to walk on, it would be a muddy mess for both patrons and store owners, who would have to clean their floors. A couple of shoeless kids with straw hats ran by and crossed the street towards a general store.

A man with a bucket of feed walked slowly to his wagon outside that store and dumped it into a large container at the back of the buckboard. He went back towards the store shaking his head at the kids who almost knocked him down.

Wilma brought me some coffee and went back to get the food.

After a few minutes, she set down the tin plate of eggs, bacon, and biscuits – with a bowl of gravy on the side. She asked if I wanted something else.

"No. I don't think so. This looks good."

Steam lifted off the plate, and it followed Wilma's dress for a few feet as she turned around and left.

At the same time, the front door opened with heavy footsteps that had sounded over the wooden boardwalk.

"Must be Clarence McCullough," one of the men said at the corner table. "I'd know them boots anywhere."

Clarence entered and nodded to everyone as he took a seat in the front corner of the room. He pulled a black scarf from off his neck, wiped his face, and put the scarf on his lap.

Mighty neat, I thought.

Wilma came over and greeted him; then she walked back to the cooking area to get the pot of coffee.

Clarence adjusted his gun and holster -- angling them away from his thick leg. His boots dug gently into the floor planks as he stretched out.

The other two men looked at him intently.

The yellow shirted man said, "Clarence."

Clarence was upset about something from the look on his face, and it must have had something to do with one or both of the men. He looked at both and said, "If we'd just known about them rustlers being around, we'd have saved them cattle."

Suede shirt said, "You know we ain't got anyone to tell us about rustlers anymore."

"Every man for himself I reckon," Clarence responded.

I listened curiously, and I wondered about the newspaper job I had seen in the paper -- this would be a great story.

Wilma brought over a plate of food for Clarence and came to refill my coffee cup.

"What happens when a man eats food this good," I said.

"He wants more. Thank you Mister. I aim to please."

It didn't take long to finish the plate as hungry as I was.

Wilma returned shortly, gathered the tin plate and bowl, and went away with her apron strings waving behind her back. I wondered if she was married, or a mother hen with several young kids. She couldn't be over thirty.

I turned to Clarence and introduced myself.

"Welcome to Kansas City. I'm Clarence, got a spread just south of here and raise cattle."

"I'm Elliot Grange and come here looking for the newspaper office. You know where the newspaper office is?"

Clarence looked at the other two men. "Them is who you want to talk to."

The man with a yellow pressed shirt said, "Papers been shut down for awhile, ever since Ralston and his boys didn't like a story that helped put him in prison. People don't like their sins advertised."

"But it's necessary to keep order," I said.

"Lets people know what's going on," Clarence chimed in.

"You got that right," I said.

"You a preacher or something Mister?" Clarence said.

"No, just looking for a newspaper job, but I can preach if I have to!"

The well dressed yellow shirted man said, "You done any typesetting?"

"No. but I can learn, and I know lots of words from my dictionary."

"Well, you certainly got the motivation. Let me think about it awhile. I'm Jim Morrisen, the editor of the newspaper office that got damaged, and I would sure like to get it going again."

"Good to meet you. I'm Elliot Grange from Virginia."

"This guy next to me is Deputy Luke Garret."

I nodded my head.

"You're a might long way from home," Garret said.

"Home is where my horse leads me, and I heard this area was beginning to grow with the new railroad and a cattle market."

"That's right," Clarence said.

"Hey, you all know of any other work around here for the time being?"

Garret said, "Mayor Hudgins needs some workers. He's building a house. Can you cut doors, windows?"

"Sure. Where can I find him?"

"The mayor's office is on the other side of the street," Jim said.

"And how 'bout a bunk somewhere?"

"Hotel's down a ways."

I don't need anything fancy, just a bunk."

"Well, let me see. He looked down at his coffee cup and back. He relaxed and sat back in his chair.

"You can bunk at the newspaper office for your work there."

"That's great. Where can I find that?"

"Well, now hold on Mister. How about a little down payment?"

"Thought you said it was for my work?"

"It is, but you aren't working yet. Besides, that place needs cleaned up after those boys ransacked it."

I bowed my head letting time take its rusty way. I'd rather work building a house than cleaning a shop, but a place to stay is a place to stay.

"Reckon you're right Mr. Morrisen. How much will it cost?"

"You clean it up and give me five dollars for two weeks; then you can start setting type after you've learned from a book there."

"Fair enough."

I reached in my pocket, took out a five dollar note, and put it on the table in front of him.

"Now. Where is the office?" I asked.

He looked at the note cautiously. "Two doors down from the mayor's office," he said as he looked over the federal note twisting it in his hand.

He reached in a pocket, took out a key, and gave it to me. "Watch out for the spider webs."

I wanted to say that was less trouble than watching out for Yankee bullets, but I didn't know what side he was on.

I grabbed my saddlebags and laid five cents down on the table for Wilma. She saw me leaving.

I gave her a wink and a smile, and I headed out the door.

9.

The sun was rising over the tops of buildings in town. Horses and dogs were kicking up dust in the street.

I waited for the dust to settle, but a team of horses passed by pulling a coach and it got worse. Then, a whirlwind came down the street and hid everything for a few seconds. I was not used to so much wind: the East had trees and hills, which blocked the wind, but here in the mid-west, there weren't many trees to block it.

Gusty winds came down the street through passageways, between buildings, and sometimes from above.

I'd have to get use to it. I pulled my hat down, collared up, and went to look for the newspaper office.

I came to a plate glass window with lettering that said *Mayor*.

I could meet the mayor later. I wanted to set my bags down and know where I was going to sleep, so I continued on and found the office that said, "Kansas City Herald".

I took the key Jim Morrisen had given me and opened the door. The office was a mess – a front window pane was missing, boards were lying on the typeset machine, and a desk had yellowed newspapers covering it. There were stacks of plain paper on the floor that were covered with dust.

But there was a wood stove on the left side of the room. It looked as if had not been damaged.

I entered and walked around it.

I needed a stove for cooking. The bottom was not rusted out, and the doors opened fine. There were leaves and wood chips sitting around its base, dust covered its top, and a lateral portion of the stovepipe was coming apart at the elbow.

I looked inside the stove and saw a ledge that could be used to warm something up – or even bake something. Good enough for cooking, I thought.

I latched the doors back and watched dust flutter in the air in the sunlight that was coming through the window.

I found the bunk in the back room. It was sitting just inside the doorway. There was a small window on the back wall, and a door to the outside. I opened the door and took a look. There was a creek nearby and a stand of trees, where I figured would be a good place to wash.

Beside the bunk, there was a wash pot and a sink. A pitcher that was half full of water sat on the floor beneath the sink.

I dropped my saddlebags on the one chair that was in the room.

I wiped dust away from the feather filled mattress that was on the wooded bed and lay down.

A couple of hours passed quickly, being the first time I'd laid on a real bed in quite some time.

I woke up a new person. I was finished with Lucille, had travelled a thousand miles, still had Yankee notes in my pocket, and now, I had a newspaper job. I did worry about Cinnamon, who looked plumb wore out from the trip.

I got up and grabbed my saddlebags. I wanted to look around town to see what kind of people were here.

A man needs to know what he's getting into before he settles down. Look before you leap, my foster mom always said.

Besides, if I was going to help build a house, get some newspaper stories, and find a woman, I got to socialize, and there wasn't any better place to socialize than the general store across the street -- where the front door was opening and shutting with people getting supplies.

I needed a hammer, chisel, saw, and a pencil, if I was going to help build a house. But surely there would be a pencil here in the office. I looked around and found one on top of a desk.

Then I walked over towards the general store.

A young lady with blonde hair in pig tails came out of the store holding the hand of a small child. They jumped upon a buckboard that fronted the store and took off down the street.

I walked in and introduced myself to the man behind the counter, who was taking canning jars out of crate and putting them on a shelf.

"He turned around and looked at me and said, "I'm Nathan Harrington. What can I do for you?"

"I need some shells for my Winchester and a new leather bridle strap, plus a few woodworking tools."

"Got those and more. The tools are at the back of the store, and I'll get your shells from a case here. Can't leave them out you know, with kids running around."

Nathan had a black mustache that twirled at it ends like his black wavy hair. His face was tanned, but showed signs of stress with wrinkles along his forehead. He had on a plain ochre shirt that looked like a bed-time shirt, with the sleeves rolled up. He wore jeans and leather shoes.

I looked around the store to see a variety of goods. There were sacks of feed for livestock, seed for gardens, and bags of fertilizer. Another section had piping, wood shingles, and tools. Another section had skillets, pans, buckets, and bags of lime.

I got a straw basket from the front of the store and picked out a few things. I found some canned goods, dried salt pork, and corn pellets. I found a few tools in the hardware section and brought them all to the counter.

He looked over the goods and started totaling up the costs. He asked me, "Where you from Mister?"

"Virginia."

"Well, that's a long way."

He weighed the corn on a scale, and put the pellets in a different bag than the one I had found nearby.

He looked at me while putting the rifle shells on the counter, probably wondering what side I had been on in the war. The war still lingered on everyone's mind, and although it was over, it wasn't over, because a lot of people lost loved ones; and some soldiers had resorted to lawlessness because they were poor. But from what I had heard just before I got in town, Confederates recently surrendered in nearby Texas.

I wanted to know more about the town, so I asked him, "How long have you been in business?"

"Been two years this July," he said with his hands on the counter.

"Looks like the war didn't damage anything here."

"The people suffered badly, losing kinfolk, but no, most kept their farms and homes, and we in town stayed in business. That'll be $2.32. The shells cost money you know."

I took out a $2.00 Federal note and a silver dollar from my pocket and gave it to him.

He looked them over and was satisfied they were real – he put both in a wooden cashbox and gave me change. He pushed the two bags of items towards me.

"Mighty obliged," I said as I picked them up. I walked across the plank floor and out the door hearing a bell ring behind me when I closed it.

And I went back to the office.

10.

I needed work now, so I groomed myself in front of a mirror and walked back along the boardwalk to the mayor's office.

I peered in the window and stopped to think about what I was getting into; I wanted to go look at the building project first.

I continued on and found the starting of a house a hundred yards down the road on the same side of the street. I stood motionless looking at it; while a stage coach behind me threw up dust that covered me from me head to toe. I hadn't learned my lesson to stay off to the side of the road when the stage coach was passing by. It was definitely time for a bath in the creek.

Laborers had finished installing floor joists, but there were no walls framed. That was fine; I could nail up walls, if there were any nails available. Many metals had been used up in the war for making cannons, firearms, trains, and rails.

I crossed the street and walked back uptown to check on Cinnamon and his stature.

Things were slowly changing in this world. This town wasn't hit nearly as hard as some, which had no supplies for building anything. A man would have to hunt native materials to make a structure of any kind.

The sun began to lower over the buildings on Main Street, and signs lit up from its brilliance: saloon, hotel, clothing, and sundries advertisements were plainly visible.

What signs had looked weathered, darkened, and hard to read earlier, now showed black letterings on white washed boards, though some signs leaned from their dried wood planks and shoddy hinging.

The traffic on Main Street had slowed, it being warmer and late afternoon. A couple fellows with bowled hats sat on a log bench staring straight ahead; one was smoking a cigar and the other one appeared to be chewing on nuts of some kind and spitting out the shells.

I nodded at both of them and continued to the hitching post near Wilma's Café.

I unhitched Cinnamon, and we walked down to the corral and a barn alongside it -- where there were stacks of hay up to the roof.

Cinnamon needed food, water, and rest. I found the livery stable attendant and made a deal with him to give Cinnamon those particulars.

He had a stall available, but warned he could not be responsible for any damage to the horse. There were a number of stallions in the corral that were anxious, and the moon was near full.

I told him to keep him separate from them.

I left the stable and went to the newspaper office feeling satisfied I had made great strides towards being a newspaper man in a small town and getting a part-time job for income.

Now, if I just knew how to set type.

Well, Mr. Morrisen wanted to get his newspaper going quickly, and he showed up the next day.

With respect about my privacy, he knocked on the door lightly, and I let him in.

"You're up early Mr. Morrisen."

"Well, son. Talking to you got me going about this paper again, so I telegraphed for some supplies this morning."

"Great."

He came inside and looked around.

"You got this place cleaned up a bit I see."

I had found a swish stick in the corner and brushed away some debris off the floor.

"Let's get Naomi, my daughter, to spit shine it a little more and get started next week." He paused and looked at the printing press and the dust on it.

"Fine with me. I also looked at the Mayor's house building and would like to help out there."

"Well, well, that's fine. Go down there and nail some boards. Be good for you until we can get this place cleaned some more."

"Okay."

"I brought you a book you can study about setting type on this machine," he said looking at the press. "Read it, and see if you can get some stories for next week too!"

"I'll do it. Bound to be plenty of stories over at the mayor's place."

"Be careful boy. You know how people can be sometimes."

"Yeah, mean and dirty. Do good to tell the public about them."

Mr. Morrisen shook his head and began to walk towards the door. He turned around and said, "I'll send Naomi over here later. She's got a key, so don't worry about being here."

"Okay Sir."

I cleaned the office some more and got myself cleaned up too; then I fell asleep after reading the printing press book, after the sun had went down, and my candle lowered.

11.

The sun hit my eyes the next morning, and shortly after I'd gotten up, I heard a knock on the door.

It was a soft knock, so I thought it to be a woman.

I had just put my old clothes back on and was sitting on the bed thanking God the war was over and for the ignorant Yankee whose horse gave me new life. And now I might have a job and some friends.

I got off the bunk, trudged through the mess of boards on the floor, and looked through the dirty window.

There stood a woman with a bucket of water in one hand, a corn broom in the other, and some rags in the front of her apron. Black pig-tailed hair was on each side of her head and thin face. She was about 5'5" tall and 110 pounds. I learned to describe people by looking at Yankee officers through binoculars and giving a good report on their physiques. They would be the first to be targeted in tents, on horses, or walking.

Her relaxed lips and steady gaze at the door said she was all business. She had on blue denim jeans with a checkered green shirt tied around her middle, which left her midriff showing. Of course, it was a warm morning.

I opened the door and said hello.

"I'm Naomi and I've come to clean this place up some."

"Your father told me you would be here. I'm Elliot."

I stuck out my hand to shake hers, and I stepped back some.

"He gave me a bunk in the back temporarily, and hopefully a job for the paper."

"Good meeting you Elliot."

She stepped inside and looked at me. "Well, this place does look a little better. You've done some sweeping."

"Have."

She laid her stuff down and looked around the room. "Daddy was never so heart broken when some rustlers damaged the equipment. This was his business and dream come true."

I stared at her, wondering what to do next, when it finally dawned on me to get out of the way before love captivated my senses and held me bondage.

"I'll get out of your way and let you go about. There's a little washing I need to do." I headed for the bunk room and grabbed my bags.

"This place sure was a mess after the invasion," she said out loud.

I yelled back, "I heard about it."

"Well, maybe it will get going again," she said.

"You work at the paper too?"

"Certainly. He's my father and we made this business with advertising and sales."

"Oh, I didn't mean to sound harsh, just thought you had other interests."

"No better interests than my father and home."

She walked around the corner and looked me over: my rangy looks, month old beard, and shaggy dirty clothes.

"You don't look like a newspaper man."

I bowed my head embarrassed. "Well, I have been on the trail for awhile. Before that, I was in the army for a couple of years."

"Well, that explains it. There's a washing place out back."

"That's just where I was headed."

I took off through the back door leaving her staring at me.

I washed my clothes in the creek and managed to get myself clean with a rag. I shaved with cold water. I stayed there while the gist of my clothes was drying in the rising sun. I admired the trees along the creek and wondered if there was any gold washed up on a sandbar.

I brushed my hair and put my outer clothes back on with my pistol tucked safely. I grabbed my leather hat, which was still slightly wet from being washed.

I felt brand new and walked confidently back towards the office through the back door to get my tobacco pouch and matches; then I headed outside to the front door area so I wouldn't bother Naomi. I sat down on the one bench that fronted the broken window.

I took the last flakes of tobacco leaves from the pouch, put them in an old yellowed newspaper wrapping, and rolled them up.

Just as I struck a match, two riders on sorrels stopped and stared at me. I nodded my head and blew some smoke towards them -- satisfied I'd got the tobacco tight enough for a good burn.

The rider in front, a medium sized man with an unshaven face, and dressed in a blue shirt and brown vest stared at me. He had on a large brimmed Stetson hat.

He said, "You're new in town, aren't you?"

"I am."

"You may not be here long sitting in front of that window."

I took a puff on my smoke and exhaled it towards the street and said, "You here to repair the window?"

Stetson looked at his partner, whose sombrero shaded his face but left the sun shining on his front side with a hand lying on the butt of his rifle.

"Kind of a smart guy, aren't you?"

"Am."

I had come prepared for such an event, with a whip cord just inside the doorway, and my pistol tucked in my pant's front.

I eyed sombrero; Stetson did not have a gun that I could see. I pulled my pistol and l laid it on my lap pointed towards the street.

49

No one said anything for a few seconds. All was quiet, as smoke from the cigar continued to waft in the air.

A shoeless boy in jeans with no shirt on ran across the street and went into a shack that had a barber pole in front of it. A couple of well dressed businessmen were on the opposite side of the street staring at the bank's front door. Clothes waved over a balcony railing on the second floor of a hotel further down the street from a soft wind that was now blowing. A a pair of red long johns caught one of my eyes while looking at Sombrero with the other.

"This place got broken into not long ago. Writing stories weren't too good for business," Stetson said.

I heard Naomi's cleaning action stop: the sounds from objects being moved around ceased.

"Good for the newspaper business – not good for the participants."

I shifted my position to allow my pistol to swing where it needed.

Stetson didn't know how to take it. He looked at Sombrero and nodded his head towards the end of the street.

"Don't get yourself hurt boy," he said as he looked at me and turned his horse reins.

No way to greet a stranger in town, I thought.

Sombrero eased off the butt of the rifle, seeing my gun turning towards him. I kept the other eye peeled on Stetson, whose mouth took on a different configuration at the sight of my pistol; he looked around to see if anyone else was watching. He looked confused when sombrero's horse turned slightly at the sight of the gun.

Stetson said nothing but turned his horse fully towards the street. Sombrero followed, while staring at me. I blew smoke at both of their hind quarters and put my gun to rest on the bench.

Naomi stuck her head outside the door and said, "You okay Elliot?"

"No. This tobacco is burning too slow and I'm low on matches."

Naomi just smiled.

"Sure," I said. "Just had a couple of visitors."

"Those were the Bellamy brothers, Roy and Jack. They work for Ralston, who got locked up after one of our stories on cattle rustling."

"Good work. But sorry the office got broken into."

"Jeopardy of the business I suppose."

She eased from the doorway and shook her hair locks from the front of her face. She opened her shirt some to get some air. A bead of sweat ran down her forehead. She took a deep breath and exhaled, while looking at some ladies across the street walking along the boardwalk; then she looked back at me.

"Well, you certainly look better. Maybe you are a newspaper man after all," she said with a smile.

"Thank you," I took another puff of my cigarette. Quietness is a virtue.

"I'll be going now. The place looks a lot better. Daddy said the book to the printing press is in the top drawer of the desk."

"I got one from him and have been reading it."

51

"Great. You got any questions, feel free to ask."

"Will do."

Naomi went back inside, grabbed her materials, and hurried out the front door skipping away.

She went to her home at the end of the street, where her and her father lived in a modest two story wood framed house that had a white picket fence around the front.

I saw her drop her bucket, broom, and rags on the porch, and run into the house.

12.

The way I heard it later, as Jim said when he came walking by the office in an hour or so, was that he was sitting at the kitchen table reading a book and she came into the kitchen almost out of breath and said "Daddy! Daddy!" And she had reached out and put her hands on a chair to brace herself.

He looked up and wondered what had got into her.

"What is it Naomi? You looked like you've seen a dead man or something."

She said, "I have, and he's come back to life. That new man you hired over at the office, Elliot: he was dead but now alive."

"What do you mean he was dead?"

"I mean he was terrible rough looking when I first saw him this morning, and nothing like a newspaper man."

53

"I think he's been on the trail for awhile."

"He went back to the creek and got cleaned up and looks like a new man. But there's something else."

"Well. What else?" Jim had asked. "You got something else on your mind. Don't go getting fresh with him. We got work to do at that place."

"No. No. Nothing like that, Daddy. Leroy and Jack Bellamy rode up to the office while he was sitting on that bench and gave him a look-down. He wasn't scared a bit, just sat there, and smoked a cigar staring at them."

"He's got some courage. May have been in the war."

Jim said he told her everything would work out in time. He told her to calm down and go check on her aunt down the street.

I was feeling right smart after I heard the story. There's nothing better than working for people that are friendly and appreciative.

After Jim left and I got tired of observing the town's activities from the bench, I went inside to see what Naomi had done, either messed up, or rearranged. A woman does not walk through a house without touching something, moving something, or laying something down.

The office was cleaned up. Papers had been picked up off the floor and stacked on a desk. A waste basket had been emptied. And all the wood splinters and residue that were in the corners of the room had been swept away.

I didn't understand why a clothesline was stretched from wall to wall though, but maybe Naomi thinks I need to wash my clothes more and have a place to hang them.

After I laid down on the bunk awhile and read the printing press book, I found that freshly printed newspapers have to hang somewhere to let the ink dry.

So much for a woman thinking about me.

The book about the Franklin press was quite informative: showing how to put rollers on, what parts to lubricate, and having a diagram of all the parts.

I absorbed a lot of it, but there is nothing better than practical experience, and I hoped Jim Morrisen would be patient with me.

Every so often, I thought about Naomi and that full breasted shirt she had on. Lucille wasn't half as good looking, and certainly not as industrious. I guessed them to be born under different stars.

I put the book down on a table beside the bunk and laid back thinking about money. I had only a few dollars left, so I got up and combed my hair and straightened my shirt for an appearance with the mayor to ask for work.

I found his office and asked him about it. He told me to go to the new house and jump in with the crew.

I went back to the office and gathered my tools. I ate some hominy from a can and some dried beef that I had gotten from the general store. I could get away with a little bit of food right now, but if I went to work, I'd have to go to Wilma's Café and get some hearty food.

On the way to the mayor's new house, I thought about that broken window. If could get a spare piece of glass. I could fix it and maybe get my $5 rent money excused.

I turned around and went to the general store. Nathan said there was an extra piece of glass outdoors in the back -- from a bar room broken window that I'd be welcome to have.

It was there, and I grabbed it and took it back to the office. I took out the old broken pane and measured the opening with my arm.

I looked at the new glass in fear, for one bad split in the pane would ruin it.

If I scored it right, it would break down the score line; and that would be fine, but glass often breaks anywhere but right.

I went out back. I scored the pane multiple times with a knife. I turned the glass over carefully and scored it some more. Back and forth, back and forth.

I stared at it again and said a prayer. Good thing I didn't have to pay for this glass or I would be trembling.

I found a log with a straight edge. I draped my shirt over the glass and set the glass down with the scored edge in line with the log's edge. I put some straw on the ground underneath where the glass would fall.

I put light pressure on both sides of the window with my hands.

A squirrel stared at me from the side of a tree about 15' up. I would have loved to shot at it but I was too nervous. I waited until he vanished before I resumed pressure on the glass.

Then I heard a crack, just one crack, which I knew was good. I was almost too scared to look.

It was okay, with a straight cut.

I had to make one more cut for the top edge, so I repeated the process and it too broke right along the score line. Suddenly, I had a window pane to fit the iron grate. I just needed some tar to make it stick.

I put the glass on the office floor and took off for the mayor's house feeling right good.

13.

I walked through the rough framed front entrance of the doorway and looked the place over.

"Hello there," I said.

One man from the rear raised himself from a nailing position and looked at me.

"Hey. I see you got some tools. You come to help?" he said.

He was a clean shaven fellow, with a red flannel shirt over a pair of suspendered jeans. A blue bandana was wrapped around his neck.

"Have. Mayor said it was alright. Looks like you all got the flooring done. What kind of walls you putting up?"

"White pine logs," another man said.

The man was older, dressed in a night shirt, also with suspenders that reached over his shoulders and back down his one piece blue cover-alls. The cover alls had a front pocket for his tools. His wavy gray hair sagged along his forehead, and sweat dripped from his pudgy brows.

While he answered, a Chinese looking man dressed in loose garb and a round straw hat was climbing a ladder trying to bend a wall stud up for a roof rafter.

I figured him to be an import that had worked on the railroad track spur.

"How big they going to be?" I asked, looking at gray hair.

"We thought about 4" x 6". What do you think?"

"Well, that'd be easier than making 6" x 8"."

"Sure it would. Axing and splitting is hard work, but pine is soft enough to get it done."

"Amen," clean face said. "What's your name?"

"Elliot Grange. I come here for the newspaper job."

"We don't print newspapers here, just do carpenter work. I'm Lawrence, cover-alls here is Mr. Richards, and that Chinese man is Shin Ho."

"Good to meet you all."

Lawrence said, "We'd sure like some help. The logs for the walls are back near the creek, but they need shaping and squaring. Can you do that?"

"Sure. How long you want them?"

"Make various sizes according to the grains you come across."

"Sounds good."

I walked out the back and over to the logs. I sat on one and began chiseling out any rough spaces -- making it smooth as possible. I made two grooves down the top side for a tongue insert to an adjoining log, which would be bound with pitch.

It would take some time to get all the logs done for the 120 foot perimeter house. When I finished two logs, the workers put some tar in the grooves and laid it on the spline of the other log – angling support sticks to the ground along the way as the wall went up.

The men started talking about digging a well and installing a hand pump, which didn't make sense to me, because the creek was only thirty yards away and there was plenty of water in it.

All it needed was a conduit to get it to the house.

"You can do that?" Gray hair asked me.

"Sure. Split logs in half and chisel a running groove along its insides and pitch or tie them together. Need a false well at the creek with a rock pile filter to keep leaves out though. Learned that from my foster father."

The three guys looked at each other, and Lawrence said, "Do it. The mayor will sure like that."

While we were talking, a woman came towards us from the opposite side of the street.

Cover-alls looked up and said, "That's the mayor's wife, Hilda Hudgins."

She had on laced shoes and a long ruffled dress that reached to her ankles.

It was a clear dry day. Mud puddles had disappeared from the area because of the warm summer air and hot sun; otherwise, she couldn't have crossed the low part of the road where she did.

Lawrence greeted her, as I sat down on a log and swatted gnats away from my sweaty face.

"I brought you all some muffins and tea."

She handed out one at a time to each of us. When I reached out for one, she said, "Talmadge told me about you. I'm his wife, Hilda."

"Pleased to meet you ma'am. I'm Elliot."

"Talmadge says you're going to work for Mr. Morrisen."

It was just what I was waiting for, and I said, "Sure am, and I'd love to do a story on this house building here. Is that okay?"

She hesitated a few seconds, thinking it over, and said, "Why I guess he won't object. It would be good for the community."

"Thank you ma'am." I took a bite of the muffin and told her the muffins and the currant jelly was right good.

The other guys were sitting on the partially built log wall eating and drinking -- but mostly staring at me – the carpenter turned newspaper man.

Mrs. Hudgins turned around and went back across the street leaving the jug of tea with us.

The day passed quickly, and I felt better than ever working at a job with good people and no one shooting at me.

That night, I read the dictionary to learn words I had never seen in the Bible. Many still didn't make much sense to me, since Bible words seemed to be more direct in the meaning in the context of a sentence.

I couldn't get enough of that newspaper though. Articles were written clear and thoughtful; and I thought I'd try to write something like them in my description of building the mayor's house.

I looked forward to next week and learning about the printing press.

When it rained in town, I hung my clothes outside on a tree branch. It was better than scrubbing them in the creek and swatting away flies and bees. I called it nature washing, and one afternoon, I put that glass in its window frame.

14.

I spent the weekend reading the printing press book, and it's a good thing, because Mr. Morrisen showed up on Monday morning ready to work.

I told him I was working on the mayor's house in the mornings, but I could come back around noon, to which he agreed. He had some rollers in his hand and went straight to the printing press.

When I got back to the office at noon, it was mighty quiet, but there he was in the corner of the room soaking ink pads. He was curing the pads with a solution mixed with urine, which I thought was a bit unusual, but he had the experience.

Between the ink and urine however, I cracked open the front door for fresh air.

I prayed for Naomi to come along with something to eat and not close the door after she entered.

At noon, in the office, I put on a work apron that was hanging on a corner post. It covered most of my britches -- something I needed when sitting down on the stool cleaning metal letters and fonts with a cleaning solution.

The sun was shining through the front window, which made it easier for me to see the lettering case before me – the capital letters being at the top, and the small letters being underneath. I stared at them wondering what to do next.

He gave me a project: I had to set type in a rack for the sentence *Today, we gaze at nature privately and quietly.*

I figured there was some kind of trick in this particular sentence, and I was right. When I had set the "p' in the rack the regular way, rather than backwards – for the printed letter to be readable and look like a "p"—I had messed up.

Jim corrected me. He said. "Not bad. But mind your p's and q's."

The work was tedious, but I finished it and I couldn't wait to see the printed page.

He loaded up the typesetting board and pressed the paper and ink padded plates together.

He hung up the sheets of paper to let them dry.

It didn't stop me from trying to see if everything looked okay. I looked at them from upside down, sideways, and up close. Seeing that I could easily get ink on my clothing, I stopped.

Jim said, "Got to wait Elliot. The proof is in the pudding."

Later that day, we took the sheet down and inspected it.

I saw a couple errors in my letter placements, and there were a couple of spacing problems; otherwise, everything looked good.

"Good work, Elliot. Now we need some stories!"

"Shouldn't be a problem with all the action around here," I said.

"No. Maybe you could do one on the mayor's house, with his permission that is."

"I've been working on that, and Mrs. Hudgins said it would be okay."

"Oh good. Naomi can go over there and draw a sketch."

"She draws?"

"Very good in fact."

"That would be great. What did you all write about before?"

"We get sheriff reports, telegraph office notes, and anything on the railroad extensions. People want to know about that. And there is an auction of cattle every month. So we find out who, what, when, where, and how. We know why, though there have been some mislabeled cattle in the pens."

"Who does all that?"

"I had a helper for awhile, but he got hitched up, and moved on. So Naomi started getting the information and doing real good. She could find out about cattle drives before they ever got here, and that's what people also want to read about; mostly because they are afraid the herds will trespass on their lands. Other people want to raise cattle and have them for food."

65

I looked out the window to see four cowboys with chaps on their legs and leather hats. Cords from their hats swayed in the wind under their chins, as they got off their horses and walked to the saloon down the street. None had a gun visible.

"People also want to know about agriculture and what will grow, so we try to give space on that too."

"So how many pages we printing?"

"One."

"One?"

"Yeah, one. One will make four if we do it right."

"I've got a lot to learn," I said.

"Don't we all."

15.

The next day started out with thick clouds covering the sky and cooler air arriving from the east.

Regardless, I put on my leather slicker and went to groove some logs at the mayor's house. I worked there for a few hours in the sprinkling rain, and then I came back to the office.

I said hi to Jim and sat down at the typesetting desk and started writing a story about the mayor's house.

Naomi arrived at the office with cookies. She looked fine - - even with strands of hair hanging down over her face. She was dressed in a soft blue blouse that was tucked in khaki pants. She had on black leather ankle boots, and a red ribbon was tied at the back of her head.

She laid the pottery bowl of cookies down on a side table, and with a leather folder in the other hand, she took out a sketch of the mayor's house and showed it to her father.

"Good work, Naomi," he said.

He had seen her come in the door.

"This will be a good start to get going again along with the story of the mayor's house Elliot is working on.

Jim went over to the press and pointed at the plate of font types; then he went to the clothes line where inked paper was drying.

Naomi looked at the paper sheet and saw a couple of sentences that were spaced well and spelled correctly.

"Outstanding," she said.

I sat in silence, knowing better than to interrupt business between father and daughter.

"Shall I show Elliot the route we take to find out what's happening in the community?"

I sat there as if I were in a new world. Months earlier, bullets were flying around me, by Yankees who were in the bushes, but here I was sitting in a building doing newspaper work with a beautiful woman and her father in a western town of the United States. Little did I know bullets had not stopped production in Virginia and were now in Kansas.

I heard them before I saw them, so I went and pushed Naomi behind a wall for protection and grabbed my pistol from my satchel near the door.

One bullet hit above the front door and splintered the top jamb. I slowly looked out the window to see two riders leaving the front of the building, on two stallions.

"Go check the rear entrance Mr. Morrisen and make sure it's locked," I said. I had Naomi locked behind me with one arm.

Morrisen ran to the back room and made sure the door was locked.

It was over as fast as it had begun. The sound of horses' hooves slowly disappeared and the shooting stopped.

Naomi looked terrified at me. "They're back, aren't they. What are we going to do?"

I said nothing but kept my eyes peeled at the front.

After a couple of minutes, Mr. Morrisen came back and said, "Well, they're finished for the day it seems. Sheriff will be here."

I calmed myself and put the pistol back in my satchel and said, "Make another good story."

"Doesn't anything bother you Elliot?" Naomi said trying to gather herself together wiping her face. She walked over to the printing press area.

"Not after being in the war."

"What side were you on?" she asked.

I walked over to my chair in front of the letter case, bowed my head, and said, "The bloody side. Now how about those cookies?"

Naomi shook her head slightly and said, "Sure."

She grabbed the bowl and extended it to me.

"I'm sorry Elliot, but events like this upset me."

"Handing out cookies? Don't you worry a bit Ms. Naomi. I'll do all I can to protect you."

"I feel it. Thank you."

"How about you showing Elliot around town and getting some news?"

"Sure Daddy. Anywhere special?"

Naomi sat down on an oak caned stool that fronted the printing press and ate the last cookie that she had a cloth under.

Mr. Morrisen stood at the window looking outside, as if fearful the shooters would return.

"No. Just the regular places." He looked at her and me. "Don't mind the Sheriff's Office. He'll be here in a minute after the shooting."

"I hope so. I'll take Elliot over to the telegraph office, the town clerk's office, and maybe we will see the cattle auctioneer, Dan Forrestor."

"Good. You all be back before long in case trouble comes back."

"Sure will Mr. Morrisen. Everything will be just fine," I said.

I grabbed my hat and led Naomi out the door and onto the boardwalk.

"The telegraph office doesn't share much with us, but when Theodore does, it's usually good," Naomi said as we made our way down the boardwalk behind the dry goods store to the telegraph office.

A dog came trotting by with what looked like a turkey in his mouth. I wondered if there were good game in the lands beyond the creek.

16.

Arriving at the telegraph office, I opened the door for Naomi and we stepped in to meet Theodore.

He looked over his rimmed glasses and said, "Hi Naomi. How are you?"

"Fine Mr. Moser. This is my friend and accomplice, Elliot Grange."

"Pleased to meet you. I'm Theodore. Your accomplice Naomi? Are you working again?"

"We are. Dad's at the shop working the press."

"Well, good for him. And I guess you wonder what's the latest."

"We do. You got anything of interest?"

"Stagecoach will be arriving before dusk with supplies and three passengers."

"That's normal news Theodore," Naomi said.

I looked around the office while they were talking. I looked at the wire hook-up of the telegraph sounder and wondered why General Lee didn't use one of those to contact another regiment to fill in the left flank at Gettysburg.

"There must be more in the last month," Naomi said.

"There's a railroad executive meeting taking place in Topeka."

"That's rather far away but still good news. What else?"

The telegraph sounder started making clicking sounds at a rapid pace, so Theodore waved Naomi off and started writing down a bunch of dashes and dots on paper.

After a minute, he looked at the dots and spaces to decipher them. Needing help, he reached behind him and grabbed a telegraph operator's code book from a book shelf. The book was coated in leather and had a coffee stain on it. He turned a couple pages to look at the meanings of some words and phrases -- and their relations to symbols.

"The Sheriff of Tulsa says a big herd of cattle is on its way to Independence -- and to be aware of rustler gangs." The date and time the message was sent was at the bottom of the paper.

Shortly thereafter, the sounder started again.

"What's that Theodore?" Naomi asked.

"Man to be hung 12:00 Saturday," he said without smiling.

"Is not. Come on Theodore, What was that?" Naomi said.

She leaned over the desk, and Theodore surely got a whiff of her magnolia flowered perfume.

He got distracted enough to tell her: "The Thomas Brothers gang of train robbers are suspected of coming towards Kansas."

Naomi straightened up and looked at me as I was admiring her ways to get information,

She smiled at Theodore and said, "Thank you, Theodore. Hope you come to church Sunday." She briskly turned around and nodded me to the front door.

"I'll try Naomi, but sometimes duty calls."

Theodore bowed his head and continued to look at the last message while Naomi and I walked out.

Outside she said, "That's good enough for that. We should have plenty of news by the time we check out the wanted posters in front of the Sheriff's office; and then, we'll go to the land's office to see who is buying or selling what."

"Is lunch on the way by any chance?" I asked.

Naomi looked as if she was caught off guard, but she regained her composure as we walked towards the Sheriff's Office. "No. Daddy was shaken up by those shooters and we should be back soon."

"You're right. Maybe another time."

She stopped in the middle of the street and faced me with hands on her hips. "Elliot, I don't know you that well right now."

"You're exactly right. I just find you rather charming Miss Naomi, and thought it'd be good to take a little break. That's all."

"Well, right now. We got work to do getting the paper ready. I suppose you being the faithful and the good man you present yourself to be will be in church Sunday morning."

"Reckon I will. Do I need to bring my Bible?"

She eased up and dropped her hands. "No, Elliot. Just bring yourself. Might get some better clothes though."

She laughed and pointed towards the dry goods store. "Right over there."

"Let's get to the land's office." And I left her speechless in the middle of the street.

She passed me on the way and walked in the door. There was no one at the desk at the moment, but it didn't stop Naomi from walking over to a wall behind the desk and looking at several postings of land claims on it.

"These are land claims Elliot," pointing to them. "The government by the Homestead Act opened up thousands of acres just west of here and people are coming from everywhere staking out portions and getting them registered."

"Suspect there is a lot of fighting over certain parcels."

"It wasn't a fair draw. Law enforcement agents, doctors, and lawyers got the cream of the crop because they heard about the offer first."

"That figures."

"It was good and exciting news though, and we sold lots of papers. I check this board weekly to see who got what and to make public notice of it as required for the certification of a claim. The land's office pays us a percentage."

74

She turned and looked for a clerk. Seeing no one, she looked at me and said, "Well, that's about it for now Elliot. Think you'll like doing this kind of work?"

"Sure, now that I know where a lot of businesses are -- and I like your father -- all business."

"He is now but he'll loosen up. Like I said, the damage to the office has really bothered him."

"I'll help the best I can."

"Elliot. You already have." She gave me a slight smile and pat on the shoulder.

"I'm going to the house and fix dinner. I will see you tomorrow. You go back to the office and check on dad."

She twisted around and walked out the door.

17.

After Naomi left, I took a good look at myself in front of the window outside the land's office that mirrored my reflection. I saw that my pants had a new hole on its side and my shirt was slightly torn -- not only from the journey here to Kansas City -- but from working on the mayor's house.

Mayor Hudgins had paid me a few dollars for the work I had done, so I headed over to the dry goods store for some new clothes.

Once inside, I saw leather boots, dress shirts, and cotton pants.

I chose a bone colored button down shirt, a pair of nice canvas khaki pants that I could use for several purposes, and a black tie with a pin. Anything fancier than all this, and I could apply for the next mayor's job.

I saw some nice black boots without spurs, but my money was limited -- maybe next time I could get them. For now, I would have to saddle soap my brown leather moccasins and make do.

The dry goods store had many items besides clothes: tarps, bolts of fabric, and even some furniture. Some used farm implements hung from the ceiling, and burlap bags were stacked high in one corner.

The room smelled of pine, and though musty, there was a homey feel about the store. Mainly it came from a wood stove sitting in the middle of the room that must have burned apple wood. It was the same type of iron stove at my parent's cabin deep in the woods of Virginia, a Mama Bear.

I met the dry goods store owner Mr. Bauerlin, who was behind the counter taking boots out of a box.

He was plainly dressed in brown corduroy pants and a denim work shirt. His jet black hair went straight back over his head, and his thin wiry frame showed he could probably think better than he could labor.

I was a foot taller than him. I laid a pair of pants, shirt, and tie with a pin on the counter.

He looked over his spectacles and counted the total amount of money due for the goods.

I gave him the money, and he thanked me for the purchase – said he would have some office supplies in soon -- after I had told him I was working at the newspaper.

I took my goods back to the office and told Jim where Naomi had taken me.

It was a good talk, and he said the Sheriff had come by and filed a report about the shooting that had taken place. "It would make a nice story," Jim said.

"Sure. Can't be scared of such events. People like to read about them."

He saw the clothes in my hands. "I see you found the dry goods store and Frank Bauerlin."

"Did. Realized I might need something if I go to church Sunday."

"People come as they are."

I went to my bunk in the back, not wanting to extend the conversation, since it was near quitting time anyway. I didn't know if he was a believer or not.

Just because Naomi went to church, didn't mean he did.

18.

Saturday morning, I got up and went to work at the mayor's house with the guys.

They had made good progress. The log walls looked good. They had been plumbed with a water level and spiked together – after pitch had been applied between them.

This morning was sunny, and I greeted the men with a wisecrack, "About time you all got working."

"We were waiting for you pencil boy, case you had to write a famous story," Lawrence said, as he was making a front door from oak slats and crossing them with heartwood planks.

"That's a fine looking door there," I said, admiring the smooth finish on its backside.

"It's dried out good and light enough to swing back and forth -- and tough enough to keep out the cold!"

"What can I do today?"

"Get us some of Naomi's cooking," Mr. Richards said.

"I ain't that friendly with her yet."

"Could have fooled us, walking her across the street."

"Might take awhile," I said.

"Getting us some food or Naomi?"

"Both."

"How about finishing some jack studs for the windows. I sawed some rough ones this morning that might work."

I looked at the window openings and saw some rough poles on the floor; they looked good measurement wise, so I said okay and went to measure the window opening and find a hand saw.

It was all I could do to keep my mind off Naomi, whom I might see at church in the morning. But what if she was with another man, or even married?

I hadn't thought of that, until after I got the invitation to church. She might have two or three men. Mother always told me that women were smarter than men. Must be, to stay out of the war.

But then mother would also say, "No venture, no gain." I was confused about what proverb to follow. Maybe she really meant, No venture, no pain.

I knew the divine plan of a man leaving his father and mother and cleaving to his wife – and to be fruitful and multiply, from what the Bible says.

But I would have to get by Mr. Morrisen for all that, which was a long way off if I didn't straighten up and act civilized.

Being in the Army, and walking up and down hills as a scout, living off the land, and fighting the enemy, didn't exactly prepare me for city life. I needed to start treating people with respect. I was rough around the corners for sure.

Dreamer and man hunter Lucille sure didn't help matters.

But Naomi was a lady -- something out of heaven I couldn't quite figure. Why would a lady like that be alone? I asked myself.

Shin Ho came over interrupting my thinking. He shook his head when I was cutting off the lip of a board with my knife.

"No, no, no," he said with his straw hat dropping to his back side and hanging by the leather cord around his neck. His red shirt reminded me of a smock I once saw a pregnant woman wear.

I looked at him with surprise and thought he was going crazy. He kept pointing at a chisel on the ground making a motion to hammer.

I shrugged my shoulders and gave it to him.

He nodded his head from side to side and smiled; then he gave it back to me, pointing at its edge.

I nodded my head and said, "Okay, I'll use the chisel if it makes you happy."

He nodded and went away happy.

I figured he had sharpened the chisel this morning and wanted someone to use it.

Fine with me.

I started hammering the chisel at the lip of the board and began thinking of Naomi again about being fruitful and multiplying, 'til I die.

19.

The next morning, I found the church at the south end of town on an incline along the creek, where I figured was a good place for baptizing people.

I got baptized one morning -- when a bullet went through the top of my hat narrowly missing my scalp in the battle at Petersburg.

I told the Commanding Officer it was time for me to get another job, and that's when he assigned me to scouting duties – its privilege not having to wear a hat and report to duty every morning. Only requirement I had was to get wind of the Yankees' movements and tell the generals.

He looked at my hat and me -- and thought better not to reject me, since I knew a couple of Generals were from Virginia.

He let me go, and after walking south a mile through the woods toward a Yankee position, I stopped at a stream trying to shake off the near miss of that bullet and said some prayers; I got baptized right there– thinking about Jacob doing a similar thing in the Bible. He thought his brother Esau was seeking vengeance against him for stealing his birthright inheritance years earlier, but in fact, Jacob was scared of his own shadow. His sin, and meeting an angel who knew how to wrestle, got him converted.

I was persuaded that God was involved with that close bullet.

The white clapboard church was surrounded by tall pines and rock mounds. I suppose the rocks had been dug out for the church's foundation. There were all kinds of rocks: dolomite, quartz, granite, and mud rocks were in piles about four feet high.

Every so often on the trip here, I'd seen mounds of rocks in open fields. People told me the Indians had made them.

I figured the Indians caught snakes in them -- and then ate the snakes. Or maybe they used the rocks to stay warm – the rocks absorbing heat from the sun. Or maybe used them for rock soup, as one my comrades suggested.

Families were arriving at the church, and most of them had walked from homes nearby, as I recognized some of them. But others were arriving on horses and wagons.

Men were dressed in their Sunday best of white ruffled shirts, black pants, shiny boots, and black leather vests. Women walked behind the men; they were dressed in corsets and petticoats, but a few had on Victorian dresses; yet others wore simple wash dresses. Some had children and babies.

A bell clanged from the side of the church grounds as I approached, and the crowd that had gathered in front began a slow march through the side and front doors as if they were going to a funeral. Most people had their heads down, as if they had had a rough Saturday night or were going to be punished for sinning. Maybe they were just tired of life.

There wasn't much joy in this bunch, but times were tough, and many people were just trying to find a meal to eat or jobs that paid money.

I concluded the crowd had sinned a lot last week and weren't too excited about hearing about it, but maybe the preacher wasn't their favorite person. Or maybe one of the members had died.

I thought about all these items as I walked near the front door.

There weren't no obituary names in the typeset that I could remember.

I entered the front door and found a flat wooden log bench to sit on in the middle of the church. That way, I could get out quickly after the service.

A few minutes later, parishioners on the bench started squirming to my left, and I looked over to see Naomi giving hi's and hugs and making her way towards me. I moved over a bit, but not too far to the man beside me.

Her father Jim went towards the front row.

Dropping her bag, and taking off a cotton sweater, exposed a dark purple corset over a gray woolen top and black woolen skirt. She had on ankle high black laced boots and smelled like white roses. She leaned over and whispered in my ear, "No need to get here too early. People want to know what the latest news is."

Words of wisdom I would remember from then on.

She sat up straight and crossed her legs looking at the people around us. She took a hymn book from the seat and put it on her lap.

For a moment, she looked at me but said nothing.

So much for modest compliments on my new clothes: she had expected them, or she wouldn't have sat within twenty feet of me.

I smiled and twitched my eyebrows.

She relaxed and waved to some people, leaned over, and talked in a low voice to others, while I wondered if we all had to stand up when the preacher came in.

We did, and everyone began to sing when he entered the sanctuary. I didn't know all the words to the singing of *Praising My Savior all the Day Long*, so I opened the hymn book beside me and figured out the title and got to the right page. Some fellow in the front pew with a deep gruffly voice led the singing.

Naomi had a soft singing voice, while I whispered the words. Me, a brute in battle, but timid in church.

After the song, and some announcements about a new family in the congregation, the pastor spoke that these times were difficult yet prosperous. He said we should all trust in God for goodness. He didn't say anything about being distracted by a beautiful woman.

A man can only do one thing at a time, and it was all could do to wonder if I was in the right place.

When Naomi patted my hand, I knew I was. My nerves calmed. I didn't know whether I should be sitting here with such an admirable woman or be in the woods hunting. Lucille wouldn't have gone to church with me if I had put a gun to her head.

Stares from other people in the church were plenty, and they iced over my shoulder. Surely there would be a load of gossip and questions, but it was nothing I couldn't deal with being an orphan from day one.

The split log I was sitting on didn't make matters any better; there were some splinters on its edge, and the stumps underneath the log, which had been dug into the ground about two feet high, grimaced with the preaching when their nails creaked.

Small spiders wandered between the log cracks in desperation to find food. One spider climbed from the post in front of me and made his way to the person in front.

After the preacher's message, a hat was passed around for an offering, the doxology at the latter part of Jude in the Bible was given, and everyone said "Amen."

People retrieved their belongings and got up slowly. Most headed directly for the front door, where the preacher was waiting to bid them farewell.

Naomi looked at me and said with a firm smile, "It's good to see you here Elliot, and I hope you enjoyed the service."

"It was interesting," was all I could mutter – because I knew the preacher had erred on several items – one being the

Lord's Prayer did not originally have a doxology ending. I could thank my foster parents for that knowledge, with all the religious books they had.

Naomi went to her father up front.

I got up and made my way to the door. I politely nodded to the preacher and shook his hand.

He asked if I was new here. I said I was, but just passing through, not wanting to divulge myself considering all the Yankees I had seen in town.

Maybe I should have been a preacher and got to shake all the womens' hands.

Naomi and her father went ahead of me out the door and down the hill.

20.

After I had left church and got to my bunk, I took a nap.

Then I had a dinner of can beans, salt pork, and some boiled wild mustard greens from a wild patch that was behind the office. After the sun went down, I did too.

When I awoke in the morning, I looked out the front window to see gray cloudy skies over the buildings across Main Street.

I went back to the bunk area, made a cup of coffee on a small candlelight stove, and put my work apron on to do whatever Mr. Morrisen wanted me to do. There wouldn't be any work at the mayor's house today.

Walking towards the front of the office, I heard loud talking across the street.

Naomi was backed up against a wall of the tack shop arguing with a man.

My senses were heightened but I was prepared for this, knowing there had to be a man in her life: she was too pretty and smart -- and a good cook too. All the ingredients for making a good wife.

One proverb had never left my mind about a woman having three men in her life: one in her words, one in her heart, and one in her arms. I reckoned the man across the street was in her words right now, but not in a good way.

The man had on a large brimmed hat and a black shirt. His holster and pistol obviously were in her words right now as she pointed at them.

By the look on her face, and her hands now on her hips, she was winning the battle. Big hat backed off and looked around to see if anyone was watching, as if he might do something violent.

I almost went outside to make my presence known, but Naomi was no pushover, and she could stand up for herself: I'd only be ostracized.

No doubt the argument was partly about me – me working with her and sitting at church together.

If that didn't get the hens and roosters clucking, I didn't know what would.

She shook off her anger with a turn of her head and relaxed her shoulders.

Big hat left with his index finger pointed at her.

Naomi looked at him when he walked away. She took both hands, drew her black hair together, and retied the bow around it. Then she smiled and came towards the office full of victory.

What a woman! I thought. I ducked away from the window quickly.

She scared me more than an accursed man would. I quickly withdrew from the area and went for another cup of coffee.

I came back to my sitting area and started adding words to the story I had written about the mayor's house -- knowing a storm would come through the door any second.

But it was just the opposite.

The door opened quickly enough but she said, "Good morning Elliot," with the breeze and words hitting my face. "Looks like rain out there today."

She hung her vest on a hook on the wall.

She had on a pearled button blue rancher's shirt, black pants, and colorful flower engraved leather boots – all set off by that red bow in her hair.

I thought maybe that she was going to get an interview with the town's board of selectmen today or something.

But there was no jewelry on her hands, which meant she might work on the printing press.

"Hi Naomi. Would you like some coffee?"

"Sure. Good time for a cup before I go over to the mayor's meeting and see what the agenda is for the week."

"That sounds like fun."

"Only if there's no arguing or unscheduled people arriving."

She sat down at the new desk that Jim had provided in the corner.

She gathered a folder and made some notes, while I got her a fresh tin of coffee.

"Sugar and cream?" I asked from the back room.

"Both, if you have it."

"I got some extra from Wilma the other day."

From the back room, I saw Naomi's forehead perk up a bit at the mention of Wilma, and I knew I shouldn't have mentioned the name.

"How's Wilma doing nowadays? I haven't seen her in a week or so," Naomi said with her head bowed.

I blushed a bit. "Fine. She serves a good meal."

I brought Naomi the tin and a cloth. There's nothing a woman likes better than to have a cloth for spills or to protect her clothing. To heck with the coffee. The napkins gets respect.

"Depends on what day it is Elliot," Naomi said, as she looked over notes.

"How's that?"

"She gets fresh food on Mondays from the ranchers bringing in meat stuffs, vegetables, and milk. If there is a cowboy group in town, it goes well, but if not, it might not get the right storage for the rest of the week depending on the weather."

Naomi moved the cloth and cup to the rear of her desk. "Thank you. You are a scholar and gentleman."

"You're welcome," I said as I looked out the window to see if big hat was coming back.

She sipped the coffee, put it down on the desk, and wrote some notes.

I admired her business like attitude, along with that black wavy hair hanging down over her ears and shoulders. And her petite form could surely mount a horse and win a race.

I looked at the font's case and started cleaning letters with an alcoholic solution that Mr. Morrisen had given me. I used a small stiff horsetail brush and dipped it in the liquid -- brushed off old ink stains and dust from the metal letters.

I wanted to talk about seeing her arguing with her boyfriend, but it could have been a private matter, and I really had no business interfering. If she wanted to talk about it, that would be fine. Maybe it was just a small issue, and I didn't need to make it any larger.

Naomi finished her coffee and got a parka off the coat rack. She went back to her desk, got the folder, put it in her arms, and stopped beside me.

"Elliot. I'm going to the mayor's office now. Father said he'd be a little late this morning."

"I hope he's okay."

"Oh, he's okay. He goes on these secret missions usually to visit someone or get a story that needs telling."

She smiled and looked briefly out the window.

I sensed her worry and said, "Okay Naomi. You need help in any way, I'll be there."

"Thanks Elliot. I'll see you later."

Without looking, I heard the door slam.

21.

Mr. Morrisen showed up shortly after Naomi left, and I filled him in on the morning's activities and the condition of the letter fonts.

He looked pleased, put his satchel down on his personal desk behind the printer, and said, "Elliot, I heard there's a cattle herd coming through the plains area in a couple days, so let's get some information about it."

"Should I go out there and wait for them?"

"Sometimes that's what we do, depending on their progress. But being in Kansas, which has a good amount of supplies and transportation East, the trail boss will send someone here ahead of time or let some of his boys come into town. We never know."

"But they're coming here?"

"Here or Independence. More than likely for rail shipment to St. Louis or Chicago. That's one of the items we try to put in the paper because there are so many people who want to know about it."

"I can understand that if the bulls come charging through their lands."

"Those herds have to eat, and they seek out the same fields every time trespassing. It's getting to be a war."

"Naomi said she was going to the mayor's office."

"Good. She's getting information at their monthly meeting."

"Takes a pretty petticoat I suppose."

"Oh, she's more than that. She knows how to dig into a person's thinking and get conversation."

"I need to learn that."

"Don't worry Elliot. She likes you. But don't ever get on her bad side, or that story will be unrivaled."

Mr. Morrisen put on some leather gloves and started adjusting some wheels at the printer stand's base with a pair of pliers.

"How about you two riding up to Oak Ridge looking for that herd on the trail? I don't like her going alone."

"Sure, but she does have friends Mr. Morrisen. She's a pretty tough lady from the times I've seen."

"Still a woman Elliot, and women need our protection."

"You're right about that."

Jim worked levers attached to the printing plates until he was satisfied the metal arms were releasing smoothly.

Across from him, I finished setting type for a story and some personal items we had received from the public: notices on equipment trades, a new business, and newlywed listings. I also placed a wording advertisement for a catalog sales company.

Naomi arrived shortly after lunch. She brought a turkey-potato dish that was steaming when she came through the door, and I lifted my head at it. Good to have a woman around.

She fixed me a bowl, and it was good -- much better than the rations in the war but not up to the roasted tenderloin of a fresh valley deer.

I didn't dare smoke afterwards in the shop with all the cleaning chemicals around.

The tobacco that I had acquired from a loaded Kentucky field would have to wait until later -- smoked somewhere at the back of the building or on the front porch.

Working here was getting me some attention -- and benefits -- like special services at Wilma's Café, good bedding for Cinnamon at the livery stable; and the fellow workers at the Mayor's new house were giving me easier work than when I had first showed up. I suppose they didn't want anything written bad about them.

And I was learning new words in my dictionary every day. One was "effervescent", which I planned to use around Naomi on that ride coming up.

In the afternoon, Naomi cleaned the office windows and swept the floor with a corn shuck broom that had been tied together with honeysuckle vine.

Small talk ensued among us, and then Jim mentioned the cattle herd.

"I'll go Daddy."

"I know you will honey, but it's getting more dangerous by the day out there. There's rustlers, angry landowners, and the hazards of nature. I've asked Elliot to accompany you."

Naomi looked at me as if a flying star had buzzed her head. She said, "Who will watch the shop?"

"I'll take care of the shop," he said.

She looked at me with a stifled grin. "Best to be in bed early tonight Elliot. It's a good ride to the ridge that overlooks the trail."

Since I was the newby around here, I could only say, "You bet. I'll be ready at sunrise."

"Well, you do ride on the trail, don't you?"

"Plenty, but never with a woman."

Naomi laughed and said, "Make sure you're horse is well fed and bring some water. There's little water on that ridge and less food."

"Okay."

22.

The next morning, I heard hooves in front of the shop. I thought rustlers may be back for trouble, so I grabbed my rifle and looked out the window.

It was Naomi's horse rearing up and wanting to sprint.

Naomi held the reins and calmed it down. She must have fed the horse well.

The sun was beginning to shine on a building at the end of the street, and there were no clouds in the sky: a good day for riding.

Naomi had on brown riding pants, an untucked dark jade shirt that slipped below her waist, and a dark brown leather vest; her hair was pony tailed in the back. Leather brown high top moccasins with tassels went up over her pant bottoms.

I was dressed and ready in my leather buckskin outfit. I had my saddlebags packed with some berries I had picked from bushes in the back, some hard biscuits I had gotten from the café, and a canteen full of water.

I grabbed the bags and my rifle and headed out the door, locking it behind me with the key Mr. Morrisen had given me.

I looked at her as she was adjusting stirrups and rubbing the horse's mane.

"Her name is Mercy, Elliot."

"Pretty horse, and from the looks of it, well fed."

The horse's thighs were well muscled and not a rib bone showed.

Mercy nodded her head as I reached into my bags and brought out a biscuit.

She looked it over, opened her lips, and with a quick motion, put it between her teeth.

"She's well taken care at the back of the house. We built a stall for her."

"Shall I get us some coffee on the way to get Cinnamon at the livery stable?" I said.

"You get your horse Elliot. I'll get us some goodies at Wilma's Café. You might stay too long." Naomi laughed, smiled, and nodded Mercy down the street.

"Meet you at the stable then," I yelled out.

I didn't know what kind of goodies she was talking about, but then I had a lot to learn about Naomi.

Whatever they were couldn't be half as good as riding with a woman who knew where she was going.

Last night, I told Ricardo at the livery stable man to have Cinnamon ready early in the morning.

Cinnamon was saddled when I got there -- all fed from the looks of his demure and front side.

I put the saddle bags over him and tied them to a blanket roll over the back of the saddle. I mounted him and made sure everything was secure, checking for tight stirrups and comfortable foot mounts.

When Naomi arrived, I fell in behind her and followed. We talked very little for quite some time, taking in the beauty of the morning and the horses finding their way along a well used hard dirt road.

After a few miles, the road disappeared into a path that started upward. I followed Naomi, turning onto the path to the south and came up beside here: I wanted to know where we were going.

"Pretty quiet out here this morning," I said.

"I like it. It's one of my favorite rides."

There were rocks strewn along the path, and the ground was hard. I looked for rocks tumbling down the hill, but none came; and the horses found their way up the smoothest part of the trail.

"Up ahead is a place we can water the horses and take a break before going up the ridge," Naomi said.

"Sounds good, but let me guess. We'll have a good look at the valley below."

"That's right. That's the Sante Fe Trail down there. Cattle drivers use it to run their cattle. If we're lucky, we'll see dust flying.'

I thought about dust flying being better than bullets flying. I was still nervous about being out in the open since the war, and I found myself looking around for strangers or Yankees.

When the trail narrowed into a one horse walk, I rode in front of her to lead as a good man would.

It was one thing to ride behind another horse, but another if a strong headwind was blowing dust off its hooves into a man's face.

And who could resist the perfume smell from a woman in the lead.

If she dropped back a little further, I might have bathed better in the creek last night.

We stopped at a stream of water coming out of the hill. Someone had dug a hole on both sides of the little stream. We dipped our hats down into the cool water and drank from them. The horses also drank.

She reached into her saddlebags and brought out a jar of what looked like apple preserves.

Being a gentleman, I took the blanket from my saddle bags and spread it on the ground. She looked at me in amazement and smiled.

"Have a seat and rest your bones," I said, as I found a boulder to sit on.

"Thanks Elliot, believe I will. Wilma sent these preserves with us," she said, holding up the jar. She dumped some on a tin plate I went and got from my saddle bags.

We ate, and they were delicious.

Looking at Mercy she said, "That saddle was dad's saddle, and it's a little hard."

She filled a cup that she had extracted from her pack and put some water and a leaf concoction in it.

"What is that stuff?" I asked.

"Chinese tea. Shin Ho gave it to me -- said it cures what ails you."

I stood up, not sure whether to sit beside her or stay where I was at -- when she patted the ground looking at me.

"Believe I will. This rock isn't soft."

After a couple of minutes, I said, "Reckon saddle's different for a woman," I said.

"Is. Needs to be wide and cushioned."

"How much longer we got?"

"Just ahead is a stand of rocks where we start to climb a bit higher to Oak Ridge. Then we can see out over the land in both directions."

"Hey, maybe we can sketch the action."

"I do sometimes, but it's difficult transferring it to metal type, and I didn't bring any paper today."

She lay back on the shawl as if she was going to take a nap.

I weren't in a mood for a nap. Her hair lay over the colored blanket as she looked at the clear sky above.

"You ever make things of the clouds Elliot?"

"Depends on what kind of clouds there are."

"Just regular clouds Elliot, like above."

"The last clouds I noticed were clouds of smoke from cannon fire and musket rifles."

"Oh, I'm sorry Elliot. That war was so bad. What did you do?"

102

"Tried not to get killed. I was a forward scout -- usually away from the action really – but sometimes the action came at me."

"Well, you made it through. And what are you doing out here."

I laughed, smiled, and said, "Same thing you are, reporting on the western frontier."

She looked at me and smiled. "I've always wanted to document things and share them with the public. My nature I guess." She lifted herself up on her arms and sipped the concoction in the cup.

We sat a while longer, but when the mosquitoes and gnats from the stream started gathering around the horses, I said, "We better get going or we're going to get eat up."

I got up and extended my hand to lift her up.

She took it, arose, and looked at me with those penetrating deep black eyes.

She paused as she stood, and I caressed her lightly to let her know how I felt.

She turned slightly around the other way and said in a soft voice, "Guess we better."

She got on Mercy and-re-tied her hair back with a bow. She spurred Mercy and said, "Beat you up the ridge," and she took off.

23.

The ridge looked out over a stretch of valley that was lush with green grass but sparse of trees.

Cattle were visible, and they were moving slowly towards Kansas City.

I could see cowboys moving slowly on both sides of the herd. There were more cowboys in front of the herd than in the back. The ones in the front were guiding the herd one way or another. Behind the herd, there was a wagon, which I figured had supplies.

"Can we get down there?" I asked.

"It's farther than it looks Elliot, and dangerous -- not only from the rocks on the ridge but any rustlers, or Indians, who may be doing just what we're doing. But now we know it's real, and it gives us something to report."

"Sure. Good to verify the news."

I looked around for any strangers on the ridge but saw none. There was mostly jagged sandstone bordering the grassy plains valley for quite some distance. I wondered if any Indians were living in the hills. Pueblo Indian cave dwellers could still be there. But certainly she was right about possible rustlers, or aggravated land owners, making trouble.

I shifted in my saddle to make sure I could grab my rifle in case I had to; yet I enjoyed the magnificent view of the valley, the open terrain, and the sun glaring off lime and sand stone cliffs.

Mercy snorted a few times -- as if to say, let's either get going or eat something here. Naomi reached down with her right hand and patted her head. She reached into her bag, brought out an apple, and gave it to her.

"Reckon how many there are?" she asked.

"Got to be over 1,000. I divided them up into groups of 50 and counted over 20."

"Well, that's what we'll say. Let's sit awhile and watch. Sometimes one goes astray and a wrangler goes after it."

"Sounds good."

I got off Cinnamon and stretched my legs. Then I brought Naomi down off Mercy, with her body still in my arms as she hit ground.

She didn't resist and clung to me as if I was her lifesaver.

She looked at me and pressed her face against my chest. I put my hands around her head and comforted her.

The wind blew softly across the ridge and turned some leaves that were on the ground beside us. Maybe our caressing did it. A waxing crescent moon was visible in the western sky from its low orbit.

"Shouldn't we tie up the horses?" I murmured.

She said, "The horses can wait." She brought her face nearer mine.

I kissed her softly on the forehead, and from there I went to her waiting lips. She was smooth, and I cradled her head in my hands and kissed her again.

It was all so calm and natural. She responded just as softly and we fit together as one.

"Reckon how many cowboys there are?" I said nervously.

"Just one right now Elliot." And she led me and the horses towards a tree and grassy spot.

We tied the horses to a cottonwood limb and I got the blanket off Cinnamon and spread it on the ground.

We lay there and kissed for the longest time.

And then there was a silence, for what seemed like an hour. We were feeling the vibrations of the cattle's hooves below, the wind, and the emotions of love that were carrying us to heights unknown. Clouds hovered lazily over the tops of trees in the blue sky.

I had to get up some, and I rested on my elbows while she nestled against my chest.

After twenty minutes, she said, "I could stay out here all day."

Her right hand went around to my left side, while I grabbed a flat rock nearby and put it behind my head for support.

"Me too Naomi. It's been nice, but we probably ought to be getting back or daddy might get worried."

She looked up at me and said, "That's what I'm supposed to say."

We had another long deep kiss, stopped suddenly -- as if God had come out of the bushes and asked what we were doing.

We sat up quickly and shook ourselves free of ground debris. We got on our horses, took one last look at the area, and the cows, and started home. There was a fresh outlook about our feelings for each other. I thought about building a house, marrying her, and raising children.

Of course, a man's best intentions often fall by the wayside when God is involved, as he kept nagging at me to preach the word. Maybe I could do both.

We arrived back at the office with the sun hitting our backs and the horses walking slowly. It was late afternoon, and I had never seen Naomi so excited at going into the office.

She jumped off Mercy, tied her to a hitching rail, and burst through the door while I stripped the gear off Cinnamon.

I could hear her, "Daddy, there's a herd coming about 1,000 head. Elliot and I saw them from the ridge."

"Slow down girl," Jim said looking up from his reading glasses from his desk at the printing press.

I stood at the front door entrance.

Naomi took off her leather hat and went into my bunk area to wash her face. I always left fresh water in the pot.

"What kind were they?" Jim yelled out as he took a look- at me.

I quieted myself letting Naomi tell the story.

He smiled, as Naomi came back in the room wiping her face. She looked at me probably wondering if I was going to speak, so I said, "Looked like mixed angus and jersey."

"Good job. I'll check out the contracts with the railroad shipper and the tax office. It's news people want to hear. What else?"

Naomi and I looked at each other sheepishly wondering what to say.

She spoke up -- knowing silence would speak its dark truth. "It was a beautiful ride out there. The ridge is a pretty place."

"How many cowboys you see?"

"I counted twenty Daddy, and they weren't driving hard. The cattle were walking slow."

Which reminded me as a reporter. I should get as much information as possible.

"Good, good," Jim said.

"We got enough information?" Naomi said as she returned the wash cloth to the back room. She emptied the pot of water out back, dipped it into a metal tub that had been set up under the eaves accumulating rain water, and came with a full pot of water. She put it on the small stand near the bunk. And she came back into the office.

Jim said, "We do. Paper should be out in a couple days."

"Oh good. I want to deliver a bunch to the general store."

Jim winked at me and said, "Nathan has always given her a treat when she takes the papers there."

I just smiled. But my mind was still at Oak Ridge Top, and a vacant ranch house that I had seen outside of town that would be perfect for starting a family. The corral looked empty, and the house doors were boarded up.

I started to ask Naomi about it but didn't want to interfere the fine day it had been.

Naomi came up to me and said, "Thanks for riding with me Elliot." She held out her hand, and I shook it, not wanting to let it go.

I said, "Sure Naomi, it was a pleasure."

She turned, picked up her hat, and walked towards the door. "I usually go alone but I thoroughly enjoyed your company."

Jim looked at her suspiciously, probably thinking something else might have happened on the trail.

I spoke up quickly and said, "Well, the sights were new to me, and I'm glad you showed me the country."

Jim said, "I'll be home soon honey. Be sure to get those taters cooking before they rot in this warm weather." He kept his head down surely thinking about Naomi and I.

"Okay, daddy."

She walked out the door and led Mercy home.

I took my gear to the back room and sat on my bunk.

In a few minutes, Jim said bye and I was alone, deep in thought.

24.

Jim came into the office the next morning area raring to go to work. He sat down at the press with his gloves on and started inking pads while I put type for stories in the right order for printing -- along with more information he had brought about the herd of cattle arriving.

After a couple of hours, I couldn't help but ask about Naomi.

He said, "Saddle sore."

I thought about that saddle of hers. Even though it was on a blanket on the horse's back -- it looked stiff and rigid. It needed oiled and softened, but then there's a chance of falling or slipping off a horse.

"I'm a little sore myself," I said.

"It's a rough ride up that ridge -- causes a person to use more muscles than ever!"

"Got that right. I've worked a horse through the mountains, but Naomi is a woman and built different."

"Might check on her about noon."

"I'll be glad to Mr. Morrisen."

"Why don't you. Take her a bowl of soup from Wilma's Cafe or something."

"Sure."

At noon, I went to Wilma's Cafe and got a bowl of chicken and onion soup with a biscuit. I humbly walked to the Morrisen's residence and knocked on the door.

The curtains peeked open, and Naomi's face appeared. She looked puzzled but waved me in.

I opened the door and saw her sitting on a velvet tufted English riveted cushioned chair in a chemise with a blanket over her. Her hair was loose and uncombed, her feet was sticking out from the blanket, and a wash pot sat empty on a stand near her. She was beautiful.

"Dad told me about your soreness and I brought you some soup and bread Naomi."

"That's so nice of you Elliot. Just lay it on the table."

"You that sore, huh?"

"It's a monthly thing too."

"Oh. Okay. Well, he's printing the paper and I ought to go back and help. Anything I can do before I go."

"Go in the kitchen and get me a spoon from the rack and a cloth from the counter."

"Okay."

I found the spoon and the cloth. And I took them both back to her. She looked at me willingly, so I bent over to hug her and give a quick peck on the cheek.

"You smell like a print shop," she said.

I smiled at her humor and let it go, much as I didn't want to. "Yes, and I better get back."

"Go ahead Elliot, and thank you. Hope to be there tomorrow."

I turned and went out the door to the office.

Jim was sitting down at his desk eating some beans from a can.

He didn't look at me when I came into the door but continued eating.

We didn't have anything to talk about, not like Yankees who talk when they don't have to. If there'd been something seriously wrong with Naomi, or the soup, that would be something to talk about. But there wasn't anything to talk about, nothing wrong with anything, and time to get the paper out.

He went home in a short while, and I retired to the bunk area.

25.

I was still in bed the next morning when I heard the front office door being unlatched.

I knew it was Naomi, from the sound of soft steps and the closing of the door.

A woman doesn't make as much noise as a man. A man will toss stuff, move things across the floor, or sit down in a chair with his feet scraping the floor.

A woman moves deftly: scared to pinch a finger, mess up clothing, or make any kind of mess. She moves slow and cautiously. That's not to say intellect doesn't have anything to do with it, because it does. A woman is way ahead of a man when it comes to being smart.

I thought more about some things.

From what Jim said, printing used to be done with wooden block letters, but thanks to Gutenberg and his associate three centuries ago, letters were made and stuck in metal to make a mold for the metal letters.

Hardware supplies for the mayor's new house still had not arrived, so the crew was taking a break. Fortunately, the roof had been covered with wood shakes, so the building was dried in.

Spring had turned into the constant heat of summer and an occasional thunderstorm. This morning, it was hot and sticky -- with a lot of humidity in the air.

Humidity swells wood; and when I looked at the walls surrounding my bunk, I saw that gaps in the wood siding had disappeared, so I knew the wood was swelling. I got up and sat on the edge of the bunk.

After prayer, I put on my britches and a flannel shirt and moccasins. I slowly opened the door to see Naomi gathering, sorting, and bundling the newspapers. At the same time, she had one paper off to the side reading it.

Today, she had on clothing I had never seen before: indigo blue pants, a yellow camisole, and quilted socks with turquoise beaded leather shoes.

She turned and looked at me and said, "Good morning Elliot. Delivery day!"

"People do like the news, don't they?"

"They do, and I do too. After all, a lot of work goes into making the paper."

"It does."

"Not everyone likes the news though, especially those on the bad end of it. But we're called to share the news good or bad as long as we write the facts. I think it's a Godly calling."

"It is."

It got quiet for a couple minutes while she was figuring out what size bundles to make. She used honeysuckle vine to tie up the bundles.

I was wondering about breakfast among other things. Now that the paper was printed, and I'd made my mark as a newspaper man, I still needed a home, a new horse, and a good woman.

It wasn't long before Naomi finished bundling the papers and I think I got the last of my requests: she came to me and laid her head against my chest with my arms curled up against her.

She said, "I'm sorry Elliot. I should have asked about you. Delivery day has always been my pride and joy. Maybe we can do something outside of work one day."

"Well. You're the one who has been sick and sore."

"Thanks to you. I healed overnight!"

"It's okay."

She turned and left with several stacks of the papers.

There was a caned chair in the office that was still damaged from the break-in months ago: a hole was in the center of the seat.

I knew there were plenty of oak splints left at the Mayor's new house from the shaving of planks, so I walked over there and brought them back to the office. I cut off any split ends, and then I cut each strip 4' long and 1/2" wide.

I put the splints in a horse trough of water outside. I smoked a cigarette until the leaf coals hit my mouth; then I took a few splints out of the water and put them on the bench.

I brought the chair outside and set it in front of me. I stripped off the old cane with my knife, and I sanded the rails.

I picked up a damp split and started weaving the warp from the front rail to the back rail – splicing it with a new strip until I got to the side rail. I spliced them with notch cuts on one end – and an arrow carved joint on the other that fit through the notch. I could have tied them together with a vine, but vine dries and will eventually break.

It took me a few hours to complete the chair.

The woven seat would have to dry a couple days, depending on the weather; then I could oil the splits and let them dry again.

This would be a good chair for someone to use. Maybe Naomi would be impressed.

Either way, I could write a story about it, and I'd be satisfied.

26.

Naomi came back in the afternoon. She told me she had delivered the papers to businesses up and down Main Street, to some private residences, and the new Chamber of Commerce, where she had left a bundle for visitors.

"How do they pay for them?" I asked.

"Some bring the money to the office. Others write it down and make payment when they have money, and yet others trade goods for them, like Mrs. Greenfeld, who gives us slabs of side meat, corn flour, or hay for Mercy. Mr. Willicot gives us oil for lanterns."

Jim had come into the office, and he said, "Elliot. Naomi keeps a record of where she delivers the papers and how many -- and whether the people have paid or not. At the end of three months, we do an accounting of them and the supplies we've used. We also document the time we've spent working, in case anyone asks us about income or loss. We like to stay on good terms with the town."

"Okay," I said. "Maybe I can learn that one day too."

"Sure Elliot, as soon as you get comfortable with the operations. Look you two. I'm on my way to the church for a deacons' meeting. There are some issues to discuss."

"Okay, daddy. Beans are slow cooking on the stove at home."

After a few minutes, Naomi said, "Something's not right with him lately. He's getting up much earlier than normal and pacing the floor, and looking out the windows."

"Could be scared for the paper. Ralston and his boys are nothing to fool around with. They're a bunch of criminals and will keep on causing trouble if something isn't done about them."

"Well, what can we do about it?"

""Well, I'm not sure what to do about it, but we'll be ready for anything they do."

But if she was worried, I was worried. That's just the way it is when a person cares about another person. Companion problems become personal problems. It was getting near quitting time, and Naomi's worry moved me to clean my rifle.

I went to the back room to get it. I got the cleaning cloth that had been soaked with cleaning chemicals and slid it down the barrel. Then I found some grease and oiled the barrel.

I plugged the end of the barrel with a bawled up piece of cloth to keep the bugs out.

Naomi fiddled with an ink pen, cleaning its tip and trying to get it to write, with ink from an ink well.

"Stick it in a little vinegar Naomi."

There was some on a shelf and she went to get it.

I worried about her and her father, and I wondered just what application to take to get the Ralstons and company out of the area. But there would always be groups like the Ralston gang.

There was a knock on the door, and Deputy Garret stepped in with a grim look on his face. He said howdy.

"Deputy," I said.

He nodded back. He walked towards me and said, "Word is out there may be trouble now that Ralston is out of jail."

"Naomi told me."

"Can't you do something to stop him?" Naomi said.

"Not til he's done something wrong."

That gave me an idea about getting the jump on Ralston -- making the first move and seeing what happens.

Naomi looked at me and smiled – conveying some kind of confidence in me that could get me killed – just for her sake.

I accepted it and told Deputy Garret I'd take care of it.

"Can't take the law in your own hands Elliot."

"How about my six-shooter?"

That was enough language to send Deputy Garret back to his office. He wasn't much of a fighter. Should have been a clerk at the Post Office with his small frame and pressed clothes and laced-up black shiny shoes. He shook his head and walked out the door.

27.

When I showed up for church Sunday morning in my new brown vest, that I had bought at the dry goods store with money I had made from working at the Mayor's house, I was sure hoping Naomi would be there.

And there she was, talking with a group of women off to the side of the walkway while a group of men were talking and standing at the main entrance.

I was wondering what was happening, because there was a lot of talk going on, and it might be a good story.

Rita Vallejo, from the new mercantile shop on Main Street, was staring at Naomi with her mouth open and jaw locked in shock.

I got a little closer to hear the conversation.

"Then what happened?" Rita said.

"They removed the body and took it to the Doctor's office," Naomi said. "Poor preacher was shot through the head."

"Well, he didn't suffer much, but his family must be heart broken."

"Sure they are. The ladies are going over to the house and help out this afternoon."

"Who's going to preach now?"

Naomi looked at me briefly. "I don't know." Her mouth turned a different angle looking at me. "The aldermen are discussing it."

I turned my head down and went to the side of the walkway as quick as I could, after seeing the way Naomi had looked at me.

Maybe I wasn't in the right place after all.

I turned again to see her looking at Rita and then at me again. Naomi waved me over and said, "Elliot. Come here. You have some religious training, don't you?"

I was stuck, so I came over and I said, "Some, but not from a church."

"Well, I don't know what we're going to do. The poor preacher is dead and there's no one to preach this morning."

She feigned her head with a sorry look I had not seen before.

I thought about a response for one second, and said, "Plenty of preachers around here."

Naomi looked me straight in the eyes and said, "But few know the word Elliot."

Naomi knew my heart and soul after our encounter at Oak Ridge Top on the blanket.

"Now Naomi. I know what you're thinking, but I don't think so. I carry a gun."

"All the more reason someone won't shoot you."

She reached over, grabbed my arm, and led me to the aldermen, who were all huddled near an oak tree.

Funny how a woman can do that -- lead a man to parts unknown – all in the name of the Lord.

But I wasn't about to let go of her.

She did, just a few feet from them as if leading cow to pasture and locking the gate. Then she gave the men a spiel about me preaching.

After a minute or so of me standing there being examined and embarrassed, they all nodded their heads in agreement.

Naomi turned me around, grabbed my arm again, and led me through the doors of the church into the sanctuary. She let go of me halfway down the aisle and pointed to the front. "It's done Elliot. Now go up there and preach so we know what to do."

Then she turned around and walked away, gathering the bottom of her dress and sitting down on a log as if the ruling mother had just given orders to her child and expected them to be done.

I took to the stage humbly, found a Bible on the podium shelf, and stood there. I waited for the crowd to be seated. They must have gotten the message about me preaching because they muddled in through the door with heads bowed.

I thought maybe I should just cancel the service, since I was now the spokesperson, and a tragedy had occurred. What a start that would be! If Naomi wouldn't tan my seat afterwards, I might have.

The people were mighty quiet, not knowing what to expect from me, especially since my gun was still visible.

When I noticed them sitting and staring at it, I took the holster off and laid it behind me on a chair.

I opened the Bible. I waited for the crowd's response to my actions. A few people reached for their Bibles. I shouldn't have to tell them to. Now, I already had the goats divided from the sheep, and I looked over the crowd to let silence do its magic. When it was so quiet a drop of water from the roof could be heard hitting the ground, I turned the Bible pages to the Book of Nehemiah, thinking about how Nehemiah built a wall of protection and a temple for worship. I concentrated on that congregation hearing the reading of the law of God and returning to obey God's law.

I read until I was ready to talk about how that reading applied to us and the town -- and how we would not let evil overtake us.

Naomi and her father stared at me, as if I was the most important person in town or something.

I sure hoped the aldermen had a plan to get a permanent preacher. I liked my freedom, I liked my gun, and occasionally I liked a beer.

But Naomi trumped all that.

I summed up the sermon with the doxology from the Book of Jude. I told everyone to have a good week, and I hoped they could get a regular pastor. May everyone have a safe journey home.

Somehow, I thought that might register with some of the crowd, who looked like their faces had turned to stone, and were locked in their seats.

That's what the spirit of God does: freezes people to think about something other than themselves or even a sermon. But I was continuing on -- stoned people or not.

I turned around and put the Bible down on a chair. I grabbed and buckled my holster with the gun to my waist, and then I walked off the little clapboard stage to the front door. Least I could do was shake some people's hands. If Naomi participated, it would make my day.

One little old lady, with a dark blue white spotted dress down to her laced black boots on her small feet, gave me a fierce look as she approached. I got ready and braced myself for the windstorm.

"Shame on you," she said. "Preaching out of the Bible and being a gun slinger. I hope your change your ways and get right with the Lord!" She pointed her finger up at me.

I said, "Yes ma'am, and you have a good day too."

She looked at me with disgust, perked her head towards the door, and walked out.

The man behind her had a different tone, "Good job young man. You work for the newspaper, don't you?"

"Do."

"Well, maybe it's time for a new job."

"At the newspaper or being a preacher?"

"You did a fine job, and I hope you come back and do it again."

"Maybe so."

I figured one liking me and one disliking me wasn't bad. Jesus had the same problem. Maybe I needed to shave closer next time for the old lady.

Naomi moved alongside me with a big smile and warm hands. She grabbed mine and said, "I knew you wouldn't disappoint anyone, except of course Miss Richards, who lost her husband in the war and has been bitter ever since."

"I figured something like that."

"How about coming over for dinner today?"

"I wouldn't miss it. You sure it's alright with the gun."

"More than alright." She squeezed my arm and walked out the door with her dad.

28.

From the minute I walked into Jim and Naomi's home, I knew the wood stove was piping hot because I felt warm air come at me.

I got there about an hour after church, after I had gone to the office and cleaned the bunk area and changed clothes. I had changed into a corduroy shirt, jeans, and some moccasins -- comfort for the afternoon.

There was also a scent of pine in the house, which I figured to be from some of the stove logs.

I said hi to Jim and excused myself; he didn't seem to be feeling well, blowing his nose more often than not, and putting salve on his face.

I walked to the kitchen -- wondering if Naomi needed help.

Naomi was busy putting dishes on the table and tending to an iron pot of beans on top of the stove. She stirred the beans with a large wooden spoon.

"It won't be long Elliot."

"Anything I can do?"

"Go sit with Dad awhile. He's still thinking about the pastor getting killed."

"He doesn't appear to be feeling well, but okay." So I went back into the living room and took a seat in the corner on the royal blue tufted chair.

Jim was sitting on the leather couch that had a walnut table in front of it. The only other furniture in the room was his writing desk and a chair that faced the front window, with a footstool near the front door.

Jim and I talked about killing of the Pastor. He said it happened because of a jealous grudge. The pastor's wife had a former boyfriend who felt Brent, the pastor, had stolen his girl from him when they were teenagers.

Since the killing happened outside of the town's limits, the county sheriff was notified. He had come and took the offender to jail.

It wasn't long before Naomi came into the room with her hands on hips and said, "Dinner is ready."

She looked tired. Sweat was on her face, and her green-checkered apron hung loose. I wondered when naptime was for these folk since everyone took one in the afternoons.

Jim and I went into the kitchen, where she had put out large wooden bowls of beans, biscuits, gravy, mustard greens, and sliced pork loin. There were slices of an onion on a smaller dish.

We sat down on the wooden chairs around the table, and I wondered who had made them.

Jim blessed the food with a short prayer and we passed the bowls around.

As Naomi passed the greens to me, she said, "Elliot. That was a fine sermon you preached about Nehemiah and the congregation. It's obvious you have read the Bible some."

I looked up from my plate and said, "My parents were great readers of the Bible; they read it every night at home."

"What faith were they?" Jim asked.

"They were Anglicans, part of a group that got off boats at the harbor in Wilmington, N.C. and settled in lower Virginia.

Jim quieted himself and dug into the greens.

Naomi said, "Well, it was very good of you to help this morning, and I hope there are more times like that."

"Are you suggesting I preach again?"

"Well. Why not Elliot? When the Lord calls you to do something, there's no other choice."

"Certainly, but I like this newspaper work and helping build the mayor's house."

"The mayor's house will be finished one day Elliot."

"It will."

"Plenty of time to think about it Elliot," she said.

Naomi could always say the right thing at the right time.

Nearing the end of eating, Naomi got up from the table and started shooing away some of the smoke that was leaking from the stove pipe.

"It's getting worse Elliot. Can you do something? Dad doesn't know much about this thing."

"Maybe," I said.

I looked at it and decided to plug the small hole.

"Maybe a nail will work," I said.

Naomi looked at the back door. "Pantry is back there. Look on the shelf for hardware. And would you mind getting some water from the well?"

"Sure wouldn't."

She pointed to a ceramic container on the floor and went to washing dishes from a small tub by the window.

I found the pantry, and some iron cut nails in a wooden bucket. I grabbed one, put it my pocket, and went out the door past a flock of running chickens to the hand pump where I filled the container with water.

I saw some mud near the pump and dug down in it with a stick to get some clay. I kept it on the stick and went back into the house.

I put the water container down on the floor beside Naomi and went to the wood stove. I wiped the nail with clay, put it in the hole of the stovepipe, and scraped some loose pitch from a pipe joint to secure the nail.

It stopped the smoke, but eventually the pipe would need replaced.

Naomi looked over and smiled. She poured the water into the tub and washed more dishes. She said, "I know it needs a new pipe Elliot, but money has been short since the paper went down."

"I understand. I'll help all I can. Hand me that container back and I'll get some water for the top of the stove. It's mighty hot in here and dry."

She did, and I went for another load of water. The house needed some humidity – especially with Jim's sickly condition. And it was a lot easier to get water when the sun was shining than tripping around in the dark at night.

Walking outside, I saw a woodpile, so I brought in a couple of logs and some kindling for the evening and set it all beside the stove on the floor.

Naomi looked over and smiled.

I knew Jim had some age on him with his gray hair and sagging face. I wanted to find out what his outlook was, so I went and sat with him again in the living room.

He wasn't in much of a mood for talking though, because he had fallen asleep.

Naomi came in and we talked for awhile, but we were all tired. I said thank you, bye, and made my way to the office bunk.

When I got to my bunk and lay down, all I could think of was having a home with Naomi: her washing dishes, making dinner, and cleaning house – not running the streets looking for stories for the newspaper. Something was driving her to do that, and then I thought about that, and where was her mother?

As I drifted off to sleep, I thought about the pastor, and why he got killed. Reckon no job is safe.

29.

Monday morning, Naomi and I were in the office alone when a person came in wanting to place an ad trying to find his mother.

Naomi looked in surprise at the fellow, but she took the information down and said she would post the item in the next issue.

But something was bothering her, and I figured it was a good time to talk about her mother, so I asked her.

She said, ""I don't know where she's at. I've searched everywhere in the county and state trying to find her, wrote stories and sent out sketches, but nothing has turned up."

"When did you last see her?"

Naomi's facial features dropped, and tears swelled in her eyes. I walked over and gave her a bandana. She covered her face with it, and for a few seconds, she turned away and blew her nose.

"She was here one minute and gone the next. I was eight years old, and all Daddy would say was that she was seen getting on a wagon and leaving with a man."

"Something must have happened for her not to come back and be with you. Who was the man?"

"After all my investigation, there was talk of her having a boyfriend. We were all having a difficult time. Daddy was not making much money writing stories and trying to sell them. And mom couldn't get along with people and hold a job.'

"Well. He's a fine man and probably did the best he could with her."

"Yes, and fortunately, his sister helped look after me."

I went back to my desk thinking about Naomi. The dinner was nice yesterday, but I wasn't ready for full-time house duties, as she seemed intent on giving me.

After the day was over, I lay down, tossed, and turned on my bunk trying to sleep.

After a couple of hours, I got a notion to have some fun. In the past, when I was indecisive, having a good time was a remedy for fixing things. It was Monday night, and the saloon was open.

I changed into my old scouting clothes of a flannel shirt and canvas pants, and I took out of the office gingerly.

A light shone through the one front window of the saloon, and I stopped a few seconds to see what was going on. I saw a few people inside, so I walked a few more steps and opened the front door to the smell of cigar smoke, cattle fodder, and alcohol.

Two women were sitting at a table next to a stairway that led to the second floor. A man was tapping the keys of a piano that was located at the rear corner of the room. The bartender was wiping the wood counter with a rag.

I nodded at him, walked across the wooden planks, and kept eyeing the women.

The Bible says something about walking into a strange woman's house is like walking into a bottomless pit, and I was wondering if I was taking the first step.

The nearest woman was in a long sleeve blue full-breasted ruffled dress. She locked eyes with me, while I stood in the middle of the room not sure what to do.

The piano man began to play a slow melody -- and blue dress walked towards me as I motioned her towards the piano man. Maybe this was some kind of set-up, but at the moment, I didn't care.

She was a nice looking lady with dirty blonde hair, plain cheeks, and a short medium build. She walked and stared at me as if she was on a mission. I checked my wallet to make sure it was secure.

I took her hands as she came towards me. I guided them around my shoulders while I put mine around her waist. She was hesitant at first, reacting to my actions – listening -- and probably thinking. Satisfied, she put her head against my chest and entered into my steps. We swayed to the music as the piano man slowly hit the keys.

The rhythm of our souls beat in unison, as we breathed lost senses to love and time.

It was too much – so she backed off and took my hands and led me to a back door – while the bartender stared at us leaving.

I succumbed to the unknown venture. I was enamored, the kind where a man can't think about what he's doing, or where he's going.

Father had warned me of this –saying following a strange woman into nowhere land is like taking coals of embers on the head that could not be cooled.

Walking through a couple of alley ways and entering into a dark one-room shack, she stopped and talked, about food, drink, love, and money.

I agreed to each of them and said I would come back and make good tomorrow, when the sun goes down, when night creeps upon its inhabitants, with men who are looking for love, in all the wrong places.

I made my way back to my bunk and wondered about the woman whose chest fell in unison with mine, for it warmed my soul, and gave life to my despondency.

30.

A few days later, Naomi came to the office to work on a story about the cowboys being in town and the herd they had driven through the grassland area at town's edge for rail shipment to Chicago and beyond.

But if she was happy about it, she didn't show it.

And I soon found out why.

I was doing everything at the front corner of the room to focus on the lettering before me -- setting type for the latest deaths that had occurred in the community -- after having been with my new friend Katy, the saloon girl, for two nights.

Naomi looked at me from her desk after being speechless for an hour and said, "You look a little tired Elliot. Have a late night?"

Right then, I knew she knew, and I said, "A little late, I suppose."

She arose from her chair with a handkerchief in her hand and said, "Must have had a good time."

I looked at her standing in the middle of the room with her hands on her hips while I was trying to decide whether I should avoid the question, tell the truth, change the subject, or get up and leave. I thought about Cinnamon and wondered if he was ready.

Before I could, she took care of my indecisiveness.

"Look at me." She paused for a second like a school teacher teaching a child. "What you do in your off-time is your business, but just remember, you're a part of this newspaper and town. When we go to interviews, we get information about the people being interviewed and not the other way around. But if you choose to make your own news, this is what will happen. You understand?"

"Yes."

"Nothing is hidden here. Everyone is grasping at opportunities to get ahead. Little birds see and tell. If we're going to get respect reporting the news, then we observe the very things we rightfully ask about."

She was really going now and took a few steps toward the door. I thought maybe she was through and heading out, but that wasn't the case at all.

She opened the door part ways and said, "Either keep yourself free from wrongdoing and unethical behavior or go find another job."

I bowed my head in some shame, and for once, I yielded to a person other than a Confederate Officer. I said, "Okay. I'll be in the right place from now on."

The door slammed shut, and Naomi walked back to her desk satisfied for the time being. Only time would tell if I could behave.

But Katy sure was sweet. Besides, befriending her got me some attention of getting Naomi for good, or at least I thought it would.

The rest of the day was awkward to say the least, and it was all I could do to think about righting the wrong.

I had misjudged her. Maybe she did like me for the future, but it would be on her terms, probably a lot more sensible than mine. There are times when a man needs to trust in something other than himself for the right way to go, or how to act, or when to do whatever. All I had thought of in the last couple years was protecting myself from getting killed. But this civilian setting was a lot different, or at least I thought it was, until the Ralstons showed up at the saloon the next night.

31.

Katy was there, but I was actually planning on saying goodbye.

Destiny, or providence, had other ideas.

It was cloudy and hot, and I was itching for a beer and some card playing.

It was a little after sunset, and I had had a good meal at Wilma's Café.

Ralston, the man of whom I had seen from a picture in an old newspaper, was now out of jail. He was sitting playing poker with two other men at a table.

He looked at me gingerly, and I got the idea to take the battle to him -- to see what would happen – before he or his boys decided to rough up the newspaper again.

I walked by the table and stared at him. After getting a beer from Ed the bartender, I sat down at a nearby table.

Sure enough, after a few minutes, he said. "You here reporting on the game or something?"

"Yeah," I said.

"How about anteing up and playing?"

I put my beer glass down on the table and said, "No."

He couldn't take my rejection. "Maybe I'll come over there and give you some news."

"You can try."

He got up from his chair and pointed his finger at me. "You write one word about me and I'll see you never write again."

"That's up for debate."

I saw Ed move from behind the door and go outside.

I put my hand underneath the table on my six-shooter, but before I could touch it, he grabbed me and took a swing at me.

I flayed the swing and hit him with a right in the gut. He lost balance, and almost fell, knocking the table and my beer over.

"Now look what you've done," I said.

He recovered and came back. I ducked his first punch but his left clipped my jaw. When he had extended his arms, I pulled his body towards me off to the side, put a foot under his legs, and pushed him to the floor.

It took him a minute to get up, while I just stared at him. As he started to get up, he was looking for something to attack me with. His gun had fallen on the floor and lay at my feet.

I was fighting defensively, but finally decided I had to knock him out if this were going to stop, and that's when

Deputy Garret showed up and told us to quit: he was arresting me.

"He started it," I said.

It didn't matter to the deputy. He grabbed me and led me out of the saloon.

"This is for your own good Elliot. His boys find out what you done, and you will be done."

Now, sitting in jail can get a man's attention. I sat down on the one bunk and stared at the iron barred door wondering when it would open again. I couldn't bear to turn around, look at the rock wall behind me, and think I was caged like an animal with no hope to get out. No, I'd look at the iron barred door and wait for it open. I'd think about why I was here in the first place, all in an attempt to start trouble with someone I really didn't know to get Naomi's attention. Well, I was sure to get that.

Maybe it wasn't such a good idea. Maybe it wasn't such a good idea to come to Kansas wanting to be a newspaper man - - find myself in different dramas and even thinking about getting married. After all, I was young, and I wanted to shoot wild game, play cards, drink a little ale, or sit on a bench looking at the people passing by.

But if a man has an ounce of talent, God ain't going to let him do that. No. He's got to benefit society in some way. I found that out writing stories and seeing them in print with people reading them.

Now, I was the story, and I wasn't too ashamed of it. It was my nature to do what I'd done. When nothing isn't working for the better, I like to make something happen, stir the pudding.

The bars of iron looked at me like a dead man, just spread out and not moving. Sometimes they'd laugh at me, and say, now we've got you, and you can't escape.

So I rested on the bunk and thought on these things. Maybe I should just go back to Virginia and be a small town newspaper man, find a good woman, and a house to call home.

Fate, or providence, as my foster father called it, don't stop a man from dreaming about something different; now, I just wanted to get out of jail.

I awoke in the morning hearing the wooden front door slam at the front of the office and my head throbbing from the one hit Ralston had given me. A little light from the moon slivered through the back wall somehow and rested on the bunk and my chest. I finally looked at the back wall to see if was really there, and it was.

Spurs clinked on the wooden floor towards me. I heard the jingling of keys in the walker's hand, and I figured it to be Garret.

He keyed and opened the iron door and just stood there. He motioned with his hand for me to follow him.

I got up, and he led me into the outer office, where he promptly told me to sit down in a chair.

He took a seat and started writing something.

I said nothing.

After he was finished writing, he handed me the piece of paper and said it was a citation for being disorderly and disturbing the peace: I could either pay the $15.00 fine or spend the week in jail.

I told him I wanted to appeal the matter.

That took him by surprise, and all he could think of to say was, "There ain't an appeal process."

"There's always an appeal process." I had learned that from my foster father's law book that was near his Bible. "Where's the Sheriff ?"

"He's out of town. Won't be back for awhile."

"There not a judge in this town?" I asked.

"Got one above the mayor's office who comes once a week to hear cases."

"Well, that's who I will appeal to."

"Now hold on Elliot. It's going to make me look like a fool if you do that."

"Didn't make me look any better you coming in the saloon and arresting me for not causing a fight."

"Ed Fenton from behind the bar hadn't come over and told me about you all fighting, them Ralstons would have carried you out in three pieces. I saved you!"

Garret leaned back in his chair looking at me.

"Three bullets in my gun Deputy. That's the problem in this town -- no one is standing up against lawlessness."

Garret cupped his hands and put his head on them -- shaking his head back and forth a little. He looked out the window -- gazing at nothing but something, maybe the empty dirty street this morning.

"Maybe we can fix this," he said.

"How we gong to fix you a keeping me locked up all night."

"I'll tell the people you was too tired to make it to your office bunk, so you came to jail."

"I don't think so. You've ruined my reputation, and I ought to be compensated. I ought to sue you."

"I'll think of something. I'll apologize in your newspaper. Give me that paper back!"

I looked at the paper with the fine listed on it and wondered if I should just tear it up or keep it for some kind of trial.

About that time, the door opened, and Naomi charged in with hair flying off the side of her shoulders and a shirt with ivory buttons on the pockets shining and khaki dungarees on her skinny legs flagging. She was wondering what was going on, because I hadn't showed up for work.

I was getting the latest news," I said.

"Sounds like you are the news Elliot. How about coming over to the paper and telling us about it. We're short on stories."

"Deputy Garret didn't say nothing but had his head bowed.

Naomi always had a way of cornering me on anything I said. I sure didn't want to lose her as a co-worker, so I said, "Okay."

She left, and I looked at the Deputy and said, "I'll take this paper with me and think about it.

Garret continued shaking his head -- as if there were lice on it.

I kind of wanted to meet the judge and town attorney, but first things first; the jail wasn't no place to sleep for more than a night.

32.

I walked towards the office to tell Naomi and her father
what had happened..

I walked in the door and hung my hat on a nearby hook. I
stretched a little with my arms, as if I had just awakened,
which I had.

Naomi and Jim looked at me quizzically.

"Well. I was just trying to get that Ralston fellow back in
jail so we wouldn't have to worry about him no more. You
know, take the fight to him."

"Well, you did that. Elliot," Jim said. "But we can't go
around making trouble in this business and be reputable and
sell papers."

"You're right. Mr. Morrisen. I won't do it again."

Naomi said, "The good Lord will deal with Ralston, just like last time. Let's stay on the Lord's side and do our business. You have to go back to jail?"

"No. Garret and I have an agreement: I won't file an appeal or sue the town -- seeing as how he hurt my reputation from being an outstanding citizen and didn't get the facts straight."

"You can file an appeal?" Jim said.

"Sure, but I'll let it go. May want his job some day." I walked to over the stand-up seat in front of the metal font's box.

"He is a bit of a chicken at times, does a lot of squawking, but never uses fists or gun," Jim said.

"A push-over ripe for criminals."

"Is."

The bi-weekly issue of the Kansan City Herald was going out tomorrow.

I asked Jim if I could go to the mayor's house after the paper was printed -- and help the guys work. He agreed to that, and a part-time schedule from now on, because I could set type faster.

I was getting itchy for something else to do for sure.

After I finished setting type for the last item in the late afternoon, I went over to the mayor's house to see how far the men had got with the building. The windows were in, along with a framed exterior and interior door.

All the logs had been used up. Wood planks covered the ceiling at top, and wood planks had been installed across posts on the two interior walls.

The men were taking a break and sitting in various spots.

Mr. Richards saw me and greeted me. He evidently had heard I was in jail.

"They let you out for good Elliot?"

"For the time being. But I wasn't supposed to be there."

"Most prisoners aren't. Some just want a good meal and a place to sleep."

Shin Ho looked up from eating noodles and took a deep breath.

"Where's the chimney for the house?" I asked to no one in particular.

Lawrence said, " Ain't got no one to build one."

"I can build a chimney."

All three of the men looked at me.

"That so. You build one before?" Lawrence said.

"Sure. My foster father and I built one on our home one summer from creek sand. There any cement around?"

"The general store has cement," Lawrence said.

I looked over at the creek. "Plenty of rocks and sand in the creek, just need a hoe mixer and trowel."

"The general store has a hoe and trowel," Lawrence said.

Mr. Richards said, "The mayor would like a chimney. Let's see where he wants it."

"Sure," I said. "You find out where he wants it and I'll build it, be best on an exterior wall."

"How's that?"

"Easy to get to."

"But a chimney and fireplace is usually in the center."

"Yes, but it's harder to maintain and get wood and kitchen utensils in and out. Besides, there are windows on the south side for heat."

"There is that. Okay, I'll ask him," Richards said.

"I'll need a ladder." I looked over at the one Shin Ho uses. He looked at me and shook his head from side to side.

He stood up and shook his head some more and started rubbing his hands down his belly looking at me.

I got the message I was too big for the ladder.

The other men gazed at him. I got my hammer off one of the shelves and took it towards the ladder. Shin Ho got all excited and shook his head no some more.

I did some language of my own with my arms, since I couldn't speak Chinese; I made notch motions with a chisel and hammer where he had nailed wood slats over the two poles. He watched me and shrugged his shoulders.

I knocked a wooden rung off with the hammer and he gasped with some language that did not sound like Chinese.

I twisted off the excess parts of the nails, laid them off to the side, and grabbed the chisel. I made cuts on both tree logs where the ladder rungs could fit, cut the wooden cross rungs to fit, and slid them in the grooves. Then I nailed them from each side.

I lifted the ladder, put it against up a wall, and jammed my foot on the bottom rung. It did not break, and I stuck my thumb up in the air at him.

He gave me a smirk.

I turned to the other guys.

"The hardest thing about building a chimney is mortaring the insides of the rock every couple feet and smoothing it out; the smoke has to have an easy escape so soot won't get all caught up in the rocks of the chimney. There's nothing worse than trying to clean out a rough chimney."

They all nodded their heads.

"And the chimney has to have a cap."

I went to the creek and started gathering rock, not just any rock, but a mixture of flat rocks for the foundation and round rocks for chimney. I gathered some thin rock for the chimney cap, large rocks for the lower part of the chimney, and a bunch of smaller rocks to anchor them all together. Shin Ho followed me and started carrying some of the rock I had thrown from the creek to dry ground.

I found a wooden bucket and dug out sand from the side bars of the creek. I brought several buckets of it back to the house and dumped the sand on the ground. Some of the sand had gravel in it, but that was alright: a little gravel in the sand would make the mortar stronger.

I gathered rock that had some roughness to it, so the mortar would stick well. Granite, white quartz, and limestone made up most of the rocks. Some had to be dug out of the creek with a pole; others were lying near the bank of the creek.

It was getting late. Shadows were lengthening along the creek from the trees overhead and the setting sun.

I was dead tired. I went back to my office bunk to eat some dinner and sleep. I was going to build a fireplace, and I hoped the blacksmith had a metal panel large enough to control the draft -- and something to fit over the chimney to keep the rain out.

I had to build a mortar mixing box, which wouldn't be much trouble -- to nail four planks together -- and set it on a few flat big stones on the ground that were mortared together.

During the next week, the ladder worked fine, after I had chiseled out a couple more spots on the posts for new rungs to carry me to the height of the roof.

I worked on the chimney for a month, despite the rain that fell for several days and having to cover up the top so the mortar wouldn't break down.

Then I assembled an iron lever the blacksmith had given me to a connecting rod for the draft plate. It would close and open it for air control. But the hole for the lever insert was way too big and it flopped around; so I slid some thin pieces of shale in the gaps and mortared them. It worked fine -- the rod staying in its place and pulling the plate up and down.

I wanted to build a fire, but not a big one, just to see if the air went to the top of the chimney. I found some pine straw at the creek's edge under some trees and brought it back to make a tepee of it at the base of the chimney. I fired it up. I watched the smoke go upwards. I shut the draft control slightly and felt heat.

Man, was I proud. Shin Ho walked in circles and danced like he was worshipping the smoke that went towards the sky.

I stretched my arms at the top of the fireplace opening, while Shin Ho looked at me. I formed them in the shape of a mantle. He got the message and went to work on a slab of oak that would be perfect.

33.

The mayor came over and liked the fireplace.

He walked around and looked at the front of it. He walked around and looked at the chimney -- that ascended the outside of the house; then he went back to the front, bent over, and looked inside. He reached his hands inside the flue and felt it; then he looked for a rag to wipe off his hands.

Shin Ho handed him a rag, and he wiped a little bit of pine ash off them.

He looked at the mantle that Shin Ho had made. The mayor ran his hands over the top and sides, as if looking for some imperfection, so he could scold Shin Ho, but he found none.

He nodded his head in appreciation and left. Shortly thereafter, he returned with a grate to fit in the fireplace for wood logs and kindling. He had even gone home and changed clothes -- now having on a flannel shirt and jeans.

All of us workers were pitching and painting walls when we saw him take to a mound behind the cabin aside the creek and try to split some logs -- for firewood.

We stared at him, and we saw he had no experience splitting wood.

The mayor learned quickly that it's not an easy thing to do. His sledge axe missed the stand-up log a couple times and slipped off the bark and onto the ground. He let out a grunt each time, the axe carrying him forward.

It wasn't long before he sat down and wiped the sweat from his face and rested his arms. His hands weren't made for swinging and cutting wood -- him being mayor and doing office work.

Cutting those fireplace logs to length wasn't easy either, working a saw back and forth. He was too prideful to ask for help, but finally, Shin Ho and I went over and looked at what he was trying to cut. Shin Ho started fluttering his arms motioning him to stop.

I saw the problem: the mayor had cut a cherry tree down and was trying to cut it up; and there's not much harder wood than cherry.

After we told him, we got a lot of respect from the mayor. Before he would try and help out on anything, he would ask us the best way to do it.

The town's folk liked the house. On evening strolls, people would stop by and examine it, oohing and aahing at some of the cornice work on the outside by Mr. Richards.

Naomi finally got over her spite of me and started talking more, but the night I had been with Katy sure set our relationship back a notch, which was fine, because I wasn't ready to settle down and get married. Naomi would have worked me to death, if not at the house, in the church to preach. Right now, Deacon Bannister was trying to preach but just ended up reading a couple verses out of the Bible and sitting down at the podium staring at the congregation and motioning for the piano player to play something.

So I examined my purpose: I couldn't go on making trouble slinging my fists and depending on my gun – maybe I was to be a man of the cloth. But then I had to listen to every little problem everyone had and tell them God knows about it and to get right with him.

And then I'd be sitting lonely because no one likes being told what to do, even when it's best for them.

Anyway, I'd rather be building something, maybe my own house, since I didn't have one. If I were going to stay here and build a house, I'd need help.

So I made the decision to stay, amidst little doubts.

Summer was in full heat with dusty streets, sweaty cowboys, and starved gardens for rain. It wasn't a good time to gather up everything and take off for parts unknown anyway. Autumn would be a better time.

Naomi was looking prettier by the day, despite her tenacity for perfection, being a newspaper snoop, and in her father's house. What did I expect anyway. There were a lot worse women in the area, trying to out dress each other, bragging about their affairs, and gossiping about neighbors.

Naomi had lots of men looking at her.

But she cared about me, more than I did. And that gets a man to thinking that he's not the best judge of himself, maybe even a bit scared of what he might find. I should be looking in the mirror.

I tried to stay out of her and Jim's house, but he was getting older by the day and losing his motivation to maintain things, and it was burdening her. If a board blew off the side of the house, she'd have to fix it. If rainwater accumulated around the yard, she'd have to clean out the ditch.

Her forehead had a crease or two, and her effervescent smile drifted to another place and time. She was worried. And one day, she let me know it.

It was early in the morning at the office and a storm was brewing on both fronts.

Dark clouds had been on the horizon in the southwest plains the past few days. The humidity was thick as molasses, and bugs seem to multiply by the day in the streets, feeding on horse crap, pig shavings, and dog scraps. Mosquitoes were breeding in puddles of water, horse watering troughs, and runoffs from the creek.

She came in the office in one of her wash dresses, a loose fitting cotton dress tied at her midriff and laying just below her knees. It was wrinkled.

Beads of sweat were on her forehead and she looked like she may have been running a ways.

At first, she said nothing, but closed the door hard and had gone to her desk.

Then with a stern face she said, "Elliot, how are you this morning."

"Fine and dandy, just brushing off these metal plates and dried up ink."

"I don't know about Dad, Elliot. He's lost his will for getting out and working."

I waited for the more talk I knew was coming. And I was not sure whether I wanted to hear it or not.

"He wouldn't come to breakfast, left food on the living room table where mice got to it overnight, and he isn't washing up like he should be."

"Well. The man probably needs a vacation."

That just started another sluice of words.

"Elliot, he's 70 years old and can barely walk here to the office. Where's he going to go? To the creek and fish? He doesn't have anyone but me. And I can't satisfy his every demand. It's like being in prison!"

"Maybe a real preacher ought to be called in for him. The deacon can't preach forever."

She gave me a stern look but came to me gently and lowered that trapeze lined head of hair.

"Elliot. Will you go talk to him and find out his intentions? He'll talk to you, I think. You know, man to man."

"I reckon, but if I got to his age, I wouldn't be doing much either."

"So it's an age thing?"

"Well sure. A man accomplishes his dreams and that's it."

"What about your dream Elliot?"

155

"Well. I'm not sure about my dream, but I like this work, building some around town, and I like the community. I reckon I've not had the dream yet."

"Elliot Grange. You preach better than any man in this town. Don't you think God has a place for you in the church?"

"Well. I shed blood during the war. Reckon that might interfere?"

"Could Elliot, but you won't know until you give it a chance. You can still build and work here, and even smoke a cigar. But you got something courageous other people don't have, and you can show us the way."

"I thought we were working on your problem with your dad."

"We were. Now we're working on your problem, which is part of mine because I like you. I've never forgot that day on the hill."

I turned slightly, thinking about some of those Bible scriptures about women – about how favor is deceitful and beauty is vain. But since neither of them were present here at the moment, so I said, "That was nice."

"Let's go again next weekend. Dad has this one planned for me cooking for the pastor's wife. She's still grieving.

"May as well."

And I knew right then my life was about to change and the dream was nearby.

34.

When Saturday came, and I was searching for something to do, I decided having a good piece of meat for dinner would be a good thing, plus, I wanted to be alone to think about where I was going in life.

It was still dark when I got up, a good time to go hunting, because squirrels and the like would be moving just after sunrise.

I got dressed and had some bottled milk that had been leftover from the previous day. I ate a corn pone that was loaded with hog grease.

I grabbed my rifle, a couple of leftover biscuits, my knife, a canteen of water, and a slice of beef jerky. I put it all in a sack and tied it around my shoulder.

I put a shell in the rifle's chamber, and four more in my pocket. I took the plug out of the end of the barrel.

I went out back and over the creek -- all the time looking for any kind of game, but mostly squirrels. I didn't feel like dressing out a deer today, but squirrel, grouse, raccoons, or coyotes would be just fine.

The day was dawning with clouds from the north, and I figured the weather to be changing from the hot humid days.

I had walked about a mile in dawn's light before I saw a big squirrel nest in a tree, and there was some rustling in the leaves nearby. I decided to go a little farther up the hill and see if there were any more nests. I could sit in the middle of them and wait until the squirrels started moving.

There was a group of three nests high above in hardwood trees. I sat down in a comfortable spot, free of ants and spiders. Two squirrels were swinging from the branches of the trees, but the sun was at their backs, and silhouettes are nothing to shoot at.

It's hard to figure where a squirrel is going. They don't always feed or go back to the nest. No. They'll stop and stare awhile and then scatter somewhere else.

I fell asleep one cold day on a log while hunting for deer – only to wake up and see a squirrel staring at me at the end of the log.

Now, at least they were moving, and the one I wanted was somewhere on the other side of a tree.

I sat beside the large oak trying to figure out where he went. I had my rifle in my lap. After a couple of minutes, I thought the squirrel was still on the other side, so I deftly picked up a small rock and tossed it to the other side.

It spooked him and he came around to my side of the tree, barely showing his head.

That was enough for me to lift the gun and shoot.

After I pulled the trigger, I didn't see him fall. I walked over to the tree and didn't see him, but the tree had a cavity in its bottom. The squirrel was sitting in it wounded and shaking, so I grabbed him and cut off his head.

I killed a couple more with better shooting, put them in a burlap bag I had brought, and put in my sack.

I wondered if I was married to Naomi if she minded me going hunting. Or would I be stuck around the home doing chores. Now, I knew what was in store for me.

If God intervened, I would be studying for a preaching Sunday morning. He knows I have seen some terrible things in the war, but the experience could help other people avoid pitfalls – and bullets.

Time would tell. It would be nice for her to cook the squirrel. I really didn't mind helping her around the house, but preaching isn't always productive, unless maybe I could get a good salary.

I had to get through these choices by next Saturday when she and I would be alone wherever.

But Oak Ridge Top could make the decision for me.

35.

Working in the same room with another person can make for a lot of emotional issues, and it wasn't no different with Naomi than with working with the guys at the mayor's house.

People get to know each other right quick, especially when someone messes up or doesn't know how to do something. Being humble will make improvements.

And that's where I was at – humbled -- without home, family, much food, or money. I was having trouble getting the ink plates closed tight to make a copy of the paper -- when I suddenly spoke up and said, "Got three squirrels yesterday."

Naomi was sitting at her desk reading something.

She looked up and said, "Great. Make some gravy out of them."

"Can you do that?"

"Sure Elliot. Pa and I lived on squirrel for a year until they all disappeared."

"I found some further up the hill -- got them in a sack in a ground dugout I made."

"Well, bring them over and I'll cook them tonight."

"Okay. Is there anything I can do for you all while I'm there?"

She looked at me like she hadn't heard me correctly. Her head did a double movement back and forth. It gave me some pause for reconsideration, but it was too late. Maybe she had something else planned, or even had a genuine boyfriend. A long ten seconds passed.

"We still going somewhere Saturday?" she said.

"Anywhere. You name it."

"I want to go to the Missouri River and go swimming, before summer ends."

"Swimming?"

"Sure. I was born there, and I want to go back and catch some fish and get wet."

"I'll have to make some fishing poles."

"Why don't you do that, and bring that Bible of yours. We can read some."

"Hey. I can't swim!"

She looked at me with a smirk. "I thought you were in the war."

"I was in the army, not the navy. I was a scout."

"Seems like a scout would have to swim. How did you get across creeks and rivers?"

"Rode my horse or took a ferry."

"Good thing you didn't fall off. Well. I'll teach you. Bring some duds."

I coughed a bit trying to slow things down but there wasn't slowing Naomi or God of the universe down. All I could mutter was, "Sure."

Well, that does it, I thought. I'm with this woman forever, and why not, the squirrel gravy will be good, but the preaching could be a different story.

There wasn't a creek big enough to baptize all the sinners in this town, unless I could convince some other men to start preaching and spread conviction.

After work, I went over Naomi's house to eat squirrel.

36.

Saturday morning arrived and I walked outside the office to the creek where there was some bamboo growing in a depression.

I figured if Naomi and I were going to a river, we needed fishing poles.

The bamboo rods were high and thick, in a low spot off to the side. The green and tan stalks covered a good portion of the ground for a hundred feet, and I wondered if the Indians had used them to shoot poisoned darts.

I found a couple of stalks that were 7' tall; and I took my knife to them and cut the fibrous stalks a couple feet up from the ground.

Then I went to the general store, where Mr. Bauerlin had some jute string and a couple of hooks. When I got back to the office, I tied a long length of jute to each pole and tied the hooks to the jute. I pierced some lead shot and put one on each line – to keep the lines stable in the water and not floating down the river.

Then I needed some bait.

I went and got a shovel behind the mayor's house and dug for worms near the creek. I didn't find any, but I did find some crickets that were hiding in a rock pile.

Naomi showed up in a multi-colored silk shirt and light brown cotton riding pants. If we were trying to camouflage ourselves from any strangers, it was not going to work. But I should remember the war is over, and I'm not hiding as a scout, though the Indians have been attacking stage coaches, railway workers, and fine citizens.

Mercy looked fit to ride, with a comfortable look on her face and being attentive to people and horses passing by on the street.

I stuck my head out the door of the office. "Be there in a minute. Got to get the bait, and my pack." I had also put a pair of pants inside the pack.

When I came back and closed the front door, I said, "You got something for lunch?"

"Sure. Chunk bread and boiled beef."

By now, people in town had accepted that Naomi and I were doing something other than just working together; but people would often stop and stare nonetheless.

We headed the horses towards the Missouri River. I wasn't sure of the way because I had come here from an eastern direction, but we were heading north.

The sun was super hot coming over the horizon. As we were riding, I pulled my hat down to shield me from the heat.

It was so hot perspiration was dripping from my face and occasionally onto Cinnamon's mane. I dried myself with a bandana every so often and looked for the next shade tree.

Naomi seemed to have no trouble with the heat; her hair was pinned up and there wasn't a bit of sweat on her.

The wind wasn't blowing, and each step Mercy took left a puff of dust rising upward – the road being void of moisture and hard as a rock.

Stopping under a tall sycamore tree to get relief from the sun, there was a group of blackberry bushes a few feet away. They were loaded -- it being late summer. There were big black berries, purple berries, and young red ones.

"Looky there Naomi."

She looked and said, "Oh. That should quench our thirst."

She got down and grabbed a jar from her pack. She emptied some of the jar's contents: a comb, brush, ribbon, and laudanum, and put them loosely in her pack.

She picked some berries and put a few in her mouth. Picking a few more, she put them in the jar.

After putting my bandana around my neck to keep me dry, I jumped off Cinnamon and picked some for myself, but I kept a wary eye out for strangers. The land was unkempt and was unfenced.

And not everyone wants blackberry bushes on their land. The bushes will take over a property and there's no way to get rid of them. There's not much of a way to get through them either, without getting pricked and scraped. The bush barbs are sharp.

But the berries make good pies, jellies, and medicines for what ails a person. The black juice makes a good stain for leather or cloth goods too.

We got going again and the path started going downhill. I sensed we were getting closer to the river.

37.

"It's not much further," she said, when she looked back at me and saw me looking around.

Cinnamon kept wandering off the path, and I figured he smelled the water or the grub in it.

"I used to come here and wash clothes, bath, get water, and fish."

"You lived not far away?"

"Our home was up the river on higher ground. But the Indian attacks made us go to town for safety. This path is the easiest way to get here, where the river turns, and the sand washes up and hardens."

Both horses slowed, because overgrown bushes had taken over the trail. We raked by several of them slowly -- watching for ticks, snakes, mosquitoes, and bees.

And then it was all clear, with the Missouri River flowing on front of us and heading south.

A side current of water was near the sandbar that Naomi talked about.

I stopped Cinnamon and looked around to get my bearings. The river was 100 yards wide. The other side had as much vegetation and trees as this one did, and there was not a soul in sight.

Naomi got off Mercy and shooed away some flies. She wiped her head with a handkerchief and grabbed her pack.

I sat in awe of the beauty of the setting: the birch tree stand on the other side, large oaks surrounding the sandbar, and the water lapping occasionally against the sandbar and rocking sticks that were floating from side to side.

"Well, Come on Elliot. If we're going to fish and swim, get the poles, blanket, and change into your duds."

"Sure thing. I was admiring the view. Something about the water flowing is calming."

"This is one of my favorite places in the county. Here, a person can think and worship the one who made it all. You bring that Bible?"

"Sure. By the way, how is your father?"

"Getting worse by the day. His sister came over this morning to sit with him. I'm not sure what's going on with him, but it's not good."

"May be his time."

"May be."

Naomi smiled and took something out of her pack. She said, "Be right back." And she went behind the bushes.

I spread the blanket on the ground and took the poles from the scabbard.

Naomi was obviously taking care of personal issues because I heard some splashing in the bushes.

When she came out, she had on different clothes: knee high loose jeans and a cutoff shirt tied at her middle.

I got the Bible out and thought about reading something about being near a river. Of course, Adam and Eve were near a couple of rivers. Maybe I ought to read that.

She walked down and began to wade in ankle deep water as though she lived in it all her life.

"Take that gun off and let's get wet. It's nice and cool out here."

I took off my holster, shirt, and moccasins. I was leaving my khaki pants on. As hot as it was, they'd dry quickly out of the water.

"I've not done any swimming," I said again, as I walked down the sandbar."

"Time you learn. Come on. I'll show you."

I walked in the ankle deep water and felt its coolness through my legs. I wondered how much debris was on the bottom, but so far, there were just a few sticks and some kind of round shells I kept stepping on.

Naomi was waist deep and loving every minute of it, splashing water on her arms, face, and hair.

"Come on. Don't be scared. You can't drown in waist deep water unless you sit down on the bottom and don't come up."

Then she giggled.

I looked at her. "Well, that's comforting. I seen lots of soldiers crossing rivers and never come back up."

"The war is over Elliot. Get your butt out here."

The last time I walked into a girl's arms for safety, it was Lucille at the boarding house when I had had too much alcohol to drink.

Naomi held her hands out and I took both. She said, "Now take some deep breaths. In, out, in, out."

She did, and I did.

"Now between each breath, hold it for five seconds."

She did, and I did.

"Now, take one deep breath and hold it in for twenty seconds. We're building up some oxygen in your body."

"How do you know all this?"

"I'm a woman. We know stuff."

I held my breath for twenty seconds, comparing myself to being near a group of marching Yankees and not making a sound.

"Very good. You are ready to go underwater. Don't worry, I'll be right here with you."

She took my hand.

"We're going down now; so take that deep breath and hold it because we're going to sit on the bottom for fifteen seconds and then come back. No kissing below!"

She pulled me down to the bottom, and I closed my eyes.

Down we went, jangled, because I panicked slightly and put an arm out to catch myself.

Then she brought me back up, wiped the water from her face and laughed -- while I gasped for air and spit out water.

"Very good. Now this time, hold your breath, stretch out, and rest your stomach on my hands, like you're going to be resting on the ground. The breath intake will keep you afloat, for awhile anyway."

"Okay."

We did, and I felt her hands slip away. I felt buoyant but all of a sudden started dropping slowly, so I put my legs out to stand up.

I came up and she said, "You got it. Now, when you start falling, just reach out and start stroking with your hands, alternating them to keep you from dropping."

I went into deeper water and tried it. After about ten minutes, I had it. I thought maybe I could make it to the other side of the river but Naomi said no, not this time. The current, though slow from lack of rain, could still take me away to the ocean and there would be nothing to stop it.

I had enough practice after gulping a third blurb of water, so I found my way to the beachhead shaking it off. Naomi was near the middle of the river swimming on top and under the water.

I kept walking on land until I stopped dripping. I wiped the water from my chest and tried to squeeze it from my pants.

She yelled from the river, "Don't sit on the blanket and get it wet Elliot. Where's the extra clothes I asked you to bring?"

"Got them. I'll change."

I went and got that ugly pair of pants from my pack and changed into them. I spread the wet ones on a tree limb to dry.

I sat down on the blanket. I was shivering slightly from the coldness of the water. A small breeze took up under the shade of the trees.

But it was all refreshing, as if God had come along and taken away all the bad things that had happened over the past few years and replaced them with something new: Naomi, the printer's job, and a place to bunk. For all that, I was thankful, and I made a vow to continue the faith journey.

Naomi exited the water and went up to Mercy. She reached up and got a towel from her pack. She went behind the bushes for a few minutes, changed into new clothes looking like a new woman. Her hair was wet and down. She twisted it to get the water out and drew it back over her shoulder.

I started baiting the poles with crickets, but a few of the crickets had died.

Naomi grabbed her pack and brought it to the blanket, and she sat down.

"Well. How did you like it?"

"Very nice. I was a little scared, but now I'm more comfortable about going in the water."

"Takes some getting used to."

She got the beef and bread out of the pack.

"How old are you Elliot?"

"Twenty-two this November."

"Oh, goodness. You are a young thing. No wonder you're restless sometimes."

"Your turn. How old are you?"

"Thirty," she said without a smile.

"Maybe you can teach me a few things."

"I don't know where life is going sometimes with Dad sick and all."

"We trust in God for goodness."

"You got that right."

We ate the provisions along with some of the blackberries we had picked.

I baited the poles with crickets and tossed the lines out in the water. I gave a pole to Naomi, and I rested mine against a big rock.

38.

We caught a few fish and put them on a stringer.

It was a good time to give thanks to God, so I picked up the Bible and read. I didn't have to ask Naomi if she wanted to hear the words – she was always ready to hear the scriptures.

"Every word of God is pure; he is a shield unto those who put their trust in him, Proverbs 30:5."

"Goodness. I hope so, with all the soldiers, cowboys, and Indians around here that get drunk and start fighting."

"Well. They're letting off steam."

"That it? I think they're wicked. Men in their right minds shouldn't act that way."

"Alcohol and a man's pride never mixed well. One will usually out do the other, and usually, alcohol wins. Luke won't stop it back in town, and the Sheriff is always on a trip."

"Well God can stop it."

"Reckon he can."

"Since you know the word, would you please start preaching Elliot? This town needs someone other than the deacon or it will end up like Sodom and burn to the ground."

"Well. I'd like to set my own house in order first Naomi. I don't have a home."

"You got one now Elliot. I'll have a talk with Dad and make sure you do. But you have to preach the word and stop running around."

"How about when you need something?"

"You can do that too."

"I do love the word!"

"Well, bring it with you!"

I'd made up my mind to preach and see what happens. See where things go. But should I put her before preaching the word. My priorities were getting strangled by personal emotions.

Reading the word comforted us, as we sat on the blanket looking at the river, overhanging trees, and an occasional boat.

One boat had three kids in it. They were dragging some kind of net behind it. Another boat had a man who was reclining at the stern but lifting his paddle every so often to straighten his course.

"Hope he don't have to paddle back," I said.

Naomi smiled. "Be a long way. You ever ride in a boat other than ferries Elliot?"

"No."

"It's an experience. Many people get sick when riding in a boat."

"Probably depends on who is chasing them."

Naomi laughed. "Not everyone is running from something Elliot. But seriously, the rocking of the boat sometimes make people sick."

"Then what do they do?"

"Either find shore or relax. Being relaxed is the key to not getting sick."

"Okay. Let's try it sometime. When I was at the Mississippi River, I saw logging platforms pass by with a couple men steering them with long poles. But that's a lot better than those ironclad boats shooting at the Confederates during the war."

"The Missouri was an important trader's route."

"Yankees took control of that and the state eventually."

I watched water twirling where fish were trying to eat the crickets. I had tied a cork bobber about two feet above the ends of both lines. When mine went down, I jerked the rod and hooked a catfish.

Naomi did the same with her pole. She caught a few bream, a sunfish, and a small bass. I moved to a spot underneath an overhanging tree thinking maybe a bed of fish would be there among the sticks. It was, and I caught some crappie. I snaked a honeysuckle vine through their gills and let the stringer into the water and put a large rock on its end on shore.

The sun was angling down past the trees, and the mosquitoes had taken up. My pants were about dry, so I went and changed back.

Naomi was lying on the blanket taking a nap.

I tied up both poles and threw out the rest of the bait.

I tapped her sleeping shoulder, and she moved slowly. She was tired; so I let her snooze a while longer. Finally, I said, "Naomi. We got to be getting back. The sun is angling down."

She looked at me like I was a stranger and murmured, "Okay. But come here first."

I leaned down and she gave me a peck on the cheek. Then we kissed on the lips.

Slowly, we got up, and shook ourselves free of debris and started loading up.

"You get more fish?" she asked.

"Did. Some crappie."

"You got them wrapped up ?"

"I'll put the stringer in a burlap bag I've brought. Should be good for the day."

"I'll cook them tonight."

"You clean them too?"

"Get yourself cleaned up. I'll clean the fish."

"A man needs to be careful what he says."

"You got that right."

39.

We were about half way home when I heard a sound in the distance: bong, bong, bong.

I thought maybe there was a salesman driving a wagon and his wares were falling off, but the banging stopped every once in a while.

"What is that Naomi?"

"The Chinese."

"Excuse me?"

"The Chinese bang a gong to talk."

"You mean like it's dinnertime."

"Sometimes. Mostly they gather after the banging but sometimes the gongs are different and no one has figured that out yet."

"Better than smoke signals I suppose. I'll ask Shin Ho."

The sound of our horses' hooves slowly reverberated over the hard trail. As we got near town, some folks on a wagon loaded with fertilizer passed us. We nodded and continued on, getting to Naomi's house right before dark.

I tied Cinnamon to a tree near the side of the house, and I followed Naomi to the rear and the shelter for Mercy. She dismounted and untied her pack.

After she had Mercy corralled in the pen, she and I walked in the back door with the burlap bag of fish and put them on the counter.

Jim was sitting at the kitchen table with his sister. He was coughing considerably.

"Hello," I said.

"Glad you all made it back."

"You've heard of trouble?"

"That area used to be crawling with soldiers and Indians shooting at each other. There two horses back there?"

"Mine's on the side of the house."

I figured I was in trouble for leading Cinnamon around the yard and near shelter without permission.

He wheezed again, and then Naomi came back into the room after having gone to the bedroom. She had brushed her hair, put on a blue printed wash dress, and looked refreshed. While I was sweaty and dirty from the ride back.

"Hi honey," he said. "You have a good time?"

"We did. The sandbar is still there and we went swimming and caught fish and got berries off the trail."

"Great."

That was enough for Jim to bow his head and struggle for another breath.

"Elliot says he going to preach," she said, as she cleaned a wash pot and took an iron skillet off a hook.

Aunt Hilda said, "That's wonderful Elliot. When will you start?"

"As soon as the selectmen approve it, if that's okay."

Jim said, "I'll motion the board to consider you Elliot."

Naomi smiled. "Elliot read some of the Bible at the beachhead Dad. He knows the word."

"Well, the church needs a preacher. People need hope and guidance. There's no better way to get it than from a preacher who knows the word."

He coughed a couple more times.

Aunt Hilda excused herself and went home.

It got quiet for a few minutes, with Naomi busy at the kitchen counter, and Jim falling asleep at the table.

"The church got a parsonage? I'll need a place to stay."

Naomi looked at me like a shot had rung out in the kitchen. But she hadn't said anything yet about where I could stay being a preacher.

Jim said, "Reckon the bunk wouldn't be good enough for a preacher, would it?"

I didn't say nothing. Naomi looked like she was going to say something but held her peace; she was mixing flour with salt and milk.

"No sir. It wouldn't. I couldn't have guests there for consultation."

"I'll take it up with the board."

"Well. You just let me know, and I hope you're feeling better."

Naomi said, "Come back for dinner Elliot. I'll have it ready in a couple of hours."

"Sounds good. Can I leave Cinnamon here? I'll be glad to pay you something."

Jim didn't say nothing but Naomi said, "Maybe we can trade for some work that needs done around here." She looked at her dad for approval, and he nodded.

"Okay, great. Thank you for the wonderful day Naomi, and I hope we can do it again."

"Come back for dinner in an hour." And she walked over and gave me a hug.

40.

I grabbed my saddlebags from Cinnamon and dropped them off at the office. I grabbed a clean shirt from a shelf in the back and put it on the bed. Then I went outside to get some fresh water, to get washed up.

River particles were in my pants, so I changed into some clean canvas ones, put on the shirt, and rubbed some magnolia flowers on me – squeezing the oil out of them onto my neck and hands. I smelled good.

I lay down for a while, tired from the day's activities. It was nice thinking someone else was cooking dinner, and I did enjoy the day with Naomi. If I got to preach at the church, so be it. I needed the money, if the congregation would contribute some.

Darkness invaded the room and I fell asleep. I woke up thinking I was back on the trail, but no, I was supposed to be at Naomi's house.

I got up quickly and walked over to Naomi's house. I hoped I wasn't late. I knocked on the door. She had an apron around her waist and a spatula in her hands when she opened it.

"Hi Elliot. It's all ready and we were waiting on you."

"I apologize. I plum fell asleep for a while."

"Understandable. It was a long ride to the river and you put out some effort to swim."

"I liked it. Maybe we can practice again another day."

"There aren't too many warm days left this summer, but it's a beautiful place to visit regardless.

The fish had been fried and were on a platter. She also had out some of the berries we picked, fried okra, and a few sweet potatoes.

It was a great dinner, but Jim didn't eat much. I guess because he was all stopped up. His coughing sounded like a pig snorting, and his breathing was being affected. He went into the living room after dinner while I helped Naomi clear the table and clean up.

"Well, this makes it a lot easier. The scraps can be dumped in the ceramic pot over there for the hogs, and we need some fresh water," she said.

I took care of both, and afterwards, we looked at each other and came towards each other for a long hug. It was time, and we were tired. I said goodbye and praised God for the day.

That sealed my fate for being a preacher, a husband, and a man of the house. No problem, I thought.

I wondered if I could arrange and conduct my marriage, since there wasn't any real preacher around.

Katy at the saloon wouldn't be pleased about me getting married, but there were plenty of men available for Katy. I'd just be another foregone conclusion.

41.

In a couple days, Jim came to the office to work on the printing press while I was writing a story about the Missouri River and its traffic.

Out of the blue, he said, "The board members approved you as preacher Elliot. But there was a mention of you visiting the saloon. Is that going to be a problem?"

"I can preach there too!"

"You know what I mean."

"No sir. Not anymore. I've given Naomi my word on that, after she confronted me about it."

"Good. She's a fine woman and in need of a good man."

"To God be the glory," was all I could think to say. "But where can I stay?"

"Try to make it here a while longer Elliot. The deacons want to provide some kind of room for any pastor who stays here or visits."

"Okay. Any particular subject they want a sermon on?"

"Peace and prosperity."

"Sounds good."

"How about starting this Sunday morning?"

"Sure."

Sunday morning was cool. There was dew on the leaves that had fallen on the ground. When I got up the hill to the church, Walt Davidson, the man who takes care of maintenance issues at the church, was there sweeping away leaves.

"Morning Walt," I said.

"Elliot."

He moved some broken limbs that had fallen off an oak tree away from the dirt path, which led up to the church.

"Got some heat on this morning?" I said.

"I fired up the wood stove a little. You preaching?"

"Am. What is the normal order? If I might ask."

"Normally, the preacher welcomes the crowd and shares whatever news needs to be shared."

Walt stood back a bit and leaned on his broom.

"Then he asks if anyone's got pressing concerns. Sometime the preacher will pray about it right then and there. Then we sing a song or two. Then he gives us a message from the Bible, passes a hat for offering, and gives a doxology and goes to the front door to thank the people for coming."

"Well, that sounds like a good agenda."

"That's normally what happens, but the people want to hear the word of God rather than a lot of normal."

"I think I understand Walt. See if I can't provide it."

"They'd be pleased."

A crowd of about 40 people came into the church and sat down on the wooden benches. It got quiet after a couple minutes, and Walt closed the front door.

Vivian Wheeler started playing the piano softly, and I took that as a cue to get the service started.

I got up from the chair I was sitting on near the pulpit and welcomed everyone to church. I looked over the crowd good. People were in their Sunday best dressed outfits of white shirts, black pants, dresses, corsets, and petticoats. Many men had on bow ties. The women had their hair brushed neatly; and some had bonnets on their heads.

The crowd quieted when I had stood.

"Good morning. I'm Elliot Grange, and the board has permitted me to preach God's word this morning. I hesitated a second to see their reactions. No one said boo, or threw something at me, so I continued on.

"For that, I am thankful. Does anyone have any pressing concerns this morning before we get started?"

A young lady raised her hand and said, "Annabelle's cow is missing."

"What's her name?"

"Who? Annabelle?"

"No, the cow."

"Oh. That's Mary Lu."

"Okay. Is there anything else?"

187

" A man stood and said, "Fred Youngblood's wagon wheel axle broke yesterday. Right when he was half-way home with a load of hay."

"Okay. How about any sick people, besides of course, Jim Morrisen, who didn't come this morning because of chest congestion."

"Hannah Cartrelle's got bad arthritis. That's why she ain't here," an older woman said.

"Well, a raw potato should fix that," I said.

That got the people loose and smiling – others stayed quiet.

"Let us bow and pray for each of these concerns."

I said a prayer for God to fix all these situations, and for a good service too. May he have mercy on everyone.

Then I took a request to sing the song: *A Mighty Fortress is our God.*

We sang that from the few hymnbooks that were on the benches. Then we sang about rising and going to Jesus, in the arms of our dear Savior, where there are ten thousand charms. It was one of my favorites.

When everyone had sat down after that song, I read part of Psalms 105: Oh, give thanks unto the Lord; call upon his name; make known his deeds among the peoples. Sing unto him, sing psalms unto him; talk ye all his wondrous works. Glory ye in his holy name; let the heart of them rejoice who seek the Lord. Seek the Lord, and his strength; seek his face evermore in Psalms 105:1-4.

Everyone in the church was staring at me, so I had their attention.

"The sermon this morning is on 2 Chronicles 14: 1-7, where there was quietness in the land. While you are turning to that chapter, I'll say if any land needs rest, it is this land, because the last four years have been destructive and depressing."

"King Asa had taken over as king of Israel. He got rid of the high places; he broke down images; and he cut down idols. As a result of these actions, and the people seeking the Lord's commandments, the land had rest."

"Now I don't know what the high places were back then in the land, but more than likely they were prideful men. And I don't know what the images were, but maybe people had drawn pictures, or maybe they were worshipping something of the earth: but the idols were cut down. These could have been carved statutes of some kind, basswood that had been whittled down and set on a shelf to adore, or maybe someone erected a pole and put a sign on it. But they were all cut down."

"Now is the time for healing. Consider what happened in King Asa's time. It's amazing what following the Lord's Commandments can do, and in this case, the land was quiet for ten years."

"Well, we don't know what will happen in ten years but we do know we can start now by being quiet and listening to God."

I waited until some murmurs, shuffling of boots, and some sniffles stopped. I waited until one person stopped moving in her seat. Maybe she was looking for attention, or more than likely, sins were arising in her soul. I waited even after I had waited, to make sure everyone was listening and God had their attention.

I let that talk about listening to God sit on the congregation for awhile, hoping to stifle the greed that was taking place in the community of trying to get ahead by taking advantage of other people.

A small baby let out a cry in the middle of the room; the mother got up and took the little one outside.

"The war in America has destroyed homes, killed family members and friends, and humiliated hard working people. But God is still on the throne. It is time to renew the vows to God and worship the one who gives peace, prosperity, and rest."

"If you don't know God's Son Jesus, who can free you from sin, and give you rest by the acknowledgment of sin, you are lost and headed for death. Now is the time to make it right."

I pointed to a lady who I knew would take my cue to sing a farewell solo.

Sally Willard acknowledged me and got up. She started singing about coming to the foot of the cross of Jesus -- whether in the valley or on top of a mountain. The sweet melody carried rhythmically over the congregation and left them staring at her and smiling.

"Come, come, unto the fountain of living waters, silently confess your sins, asking God to forgive you, through the blood of Jesus, to free your soul . . . to free your soul -- glorify God . . . who loves you."

There wasn't much more I could add to that, so I read the doxology in Jude and closed the session.

Well, Naomi was in the front seat sniffling and crying. I thought maybe she was sitting on a splinter of wood or something. Or maybe she hadn't been right with the Lord after all. Or maybe she was just happy. Hard to tell about a woman.

I hurried to the front door and gave thanks to each person that had come. Some said it was a good sermon and hoped I'd preach again.

I thanked Sally for singing that song. I thanked Walt Davidson for indoctrinating me. And I thanked God for completing the service in accordance with his word.

42.

I looked back from the front door and saw Naomi talking with two other ladies. I figured it was about Jim being sick, or it could be about my preaching.

I was beginning to feel like Naomi was my security blanket or something – slowly – gradually building confidence with her. I did want to make sure she got home alright.

After the congregation had left, she came to the doorway and said, "That sermon was real nice Elliot. Della and Vivian loved it. They both think you will make a great pastor."

"Pleased to hear that. May I escort you home."

"You may."

I saw Walt tidying up the church, looking for any left over goods, and straightening the hymn books neatly on the seats.

I figured him to lock the church door, since he was the one who opened it. A preacher can only do so much.

"Naomi and I walked down the trail and around the corner of Main Street to her home.

Once we arrived at the front steps, she said, "Thank you Elliot. I think I'll go inside, see how Dad is doing, and rest awhile. He was up a lot last night wheezing."

"Sure thing. You need me, come get me. I might look for a little gold in the creek this afternoon."

Naomi smiled and said, "Find a lode stone and don't be fooled by false gold."

"Okay Naomi. I'm on the right path now. I just needed some direction, that's all."

"Oh, good to hear that! Come by later if you feel like it. Need some rest right now."

"See you tomorrow at work. Have a good afternoon."

I went to my bunk at the office and took a nap. I woke up thinking about Jim's poor condition, the church, the newspaper, and Naomi. She was a wonderful woman, focused on keeping house, watching her father, going to church, and working in the community.

What more could I ask?

But was I good enough. The more I thought about it, I knew I wasn't. I hoped the Lord would help me. The secret was being obedient, and I thought about the scripture of a man giving honor to the wife and nurturing her to godliness. Like Jesus, who loved humanity and gave his life for all of it.

I think I could do that for Naomi, but I would have to pray about it a lot. I'd been spending years trying to save my own life.

God had brought me this far, and I wasn't exactly in dire straits with no food, money, or shelter. So I lay there and gave thanks. And I thought about that gold: I'd need a screen, pan, and a small shovel.

And then a deep sleep fell upon me, one I don't where it came from. Maybe it was the weather, maybe all my nervousness and stress from life suddenly left, or maybe God himself decided to come down and bring this heaviness on me. He did that to a couple of people in the Bible, and they were given ultimatums and missions. The second I could deal with, the first might be difficult.

I dreamed of finding a large gold nugget, not in the creek, but in a quartz vein on a ridge. I chipped and hammered away at it. I beat it with a chisel and another quartz rock. I was sweating heavy, and my heart was racing, because I was going to be rich. But the whole time someone was watching me, and when I finally got the nugget out, it was taken away by a stranger. Right then, I knew it was about Naomi, and I'd better get her quick.

And that's the feeling I woke up with.

43.

"Where's your father?" I asked Naomi in the morning in the office.

"He's not going to make it."

"To the office, or for good."

"I'm not sure he'll be able to work any longer. You think you can handle the printing?"

"I think so. May have to ask him a few questions about mixing them chemicals."

"Let's do it. How many got stories we got?"

I walked over to my desk and saw three had been written: one on the mayor's chimney, me the new pastor at church, and a live acting show coming to town. There were other tidbits of information for the paper: a cow roping contest, a new judge for the territory, and Salt Lake City being the final link for a telegraph line to California.

I told Naomi what we had.

She said, "That's more than enough, with the land deals and arrests. Save something for next time if you can."

"Sure."

"You find any gold?"

"Plenty in my dream."

"You think it's real?"

"You bet."

"Hope it's a big nugget worth a thousand dollars."

"It's worth more than that."

She bowed her head and looked into a book of photographs that a new business in town had given her.

"Naomi." She looked over at me in wonderment."

"You ever think about getting married one day?"

Naomi just laughed. "Why certainly Elliot. It's every woman's dream to find the right man and enjoy the pleasures of life."

"I haven't never been married. You?"

"Well, I haven't told you this, but I had a brief ceremony when I was young that didn't work out: I was abandoned. So I just figured I was supposed to be with dad until God brought me someone. I sure didn't pick the right one."

I choked up a bit and took a deep breath. I stayed right where I was, standing near my desk. "Maybe God has."

She looked up and said, "Elliot Grange. Are you proposing to me?"

"Maybe. A little bit."

"Well, Are you or aren't you?"

"Well. I guess I am."

"You can't guess about it. You need to be sure of what you're getting into. It's a responsibility having a wife."

"Naomi. I'm prepared to take it and love you the rest of my life.

She got up from her chair and came to me. ""You sure you want a woman near old as your mother?"

"More than sure."

"Maybe we ought to give it some time?"

"It's been six months." I leaned down towards her, and I said, "How about five seconds?"

She could resist it no longer. We held each other and kissed for a long time.

She broke away and said, "You don't mind bringing in firewood, boarding the horses, fixing food, and putting up with my jabber? And what about Dad?"

"I think he'll be pleased. The rest will take care of itself."

"You know. You're right. Okay! Go swimming with me again?"

"Sure, if you'll go gold digging with me."

Naomi smiled and gave me another kiss and hug.

"Hey, we got to put an announcement for the paper!" she said.

"Amen."

We set the date for late October when the weather gets cold and couples want to hibernate, when the harvest is stored, the animals are bedding, and the rains fall making sleep.

Naomi went home for lunch and came back talking about Jim. "He's taken a turn for the worse Elliot. What can we do?"

197

"What did Doctor Finklemeier say?"

"Said he was all stopped up."

"That's easy to fix with a few prunes and coffee. What did the doc do?"

"Gave him some kind of alcohol medicine. Said it would relieve his pain."

"Finklemeier don't know. Jim needs something to run whatever it is out of him."

"Would you please go fix him?"

"Think he'll listen?"

"Sure. A man tends to listen better when he's hurting."

"You know. I think you're right. Okay, I'll fix up a potion and take it over there. Be good to have a pone with it."

"Go to Wilma's Cafe and get one, maybe take some soup too."

"That'll work."

I went and got some dried prunes at the general store; then I went to the café. Wilma gladly gave me a couple corn pones and a bowl of chicken soup, but she wanted the bowl back. She said the Indians from Oklahoma kept stealing her utensils, plates, and bowls. I thought Indians made their own bowls.

Jim was covered up on his favorite chair even though the day was hot and clammy. I call that being insecure and sick; nevertheless, I approached him with the potions.

"Got something for you," I said.

"I need something. Can't hardly breathe or move."

"Might have a bad bite or something."

"Let me see that."

198

"Suggest you eat a couple of these dried prunes, get your bowels relieved."

"Soup looks good."

"Well. Have it your way. I'll just lay this all down here on the table and let you pick."

"Finklemeier says the weather here in the winter is bad for me."

"Right good if a person hasn't got anywhere else to go."

"Is, but I got a cousin in Arizona. He writes and says the air there is light: enough a man can breathe."

"Well. That's an option. Don't know if Naomi will like that."

"You and her get along good."

"We do, and I'll watch over her."

"All them chemicals in the shop may be making me sick."

"Maybe. I always open the door or window when the bottles are opened or the paper is drying."

"Think you can handle the paper?"

"Sure, with Naomi as boss."

"It's settled then."

44.

After a couple days, Jim felt much better, but Finklemeier said there was some kind of lump around his lungs. I knew Jim wouldn't let me take a hammer to it, so I let go of the healing business since he wasn't going to do exactly what I prescribed anyway.

The next day Naomi said, "What do you think of Finklemeier's diagnosis and that lump Elliot."

"Anything can be fixed."

"Dad won't let you, will he?"

"No. His pride won't allow him. No sweat lodge for him."

"I know you're right. There isn't no sense squeezing juice from a dry pear."

"Men got to learn on their own. A change will do him good."

"He's talking about moving to a cousin's house in Arizona."

"He told me. Be good for him to breath that dry air if the dust storms don't kill him."

"We got to adapt to our situations."

"Do. But he won't, and he won't leave until he knows you're taken care of. I told him I'd watch over you and not to worry."

"People are getting excited about us getting married, but who will marry us?"

"Reckon I will."

Naomi laughed a bit.

"I think we have to have a man who is an ordained minister Elliot."

"Well. How do we do that?"

"Go over to the mayor's office and get a piece of paper and put it down you're a minister by unanimous consent of the board members; then file it in the court. Still, we would have to find one who is -- maybe in the next county."

"There's a Catholic church at Lawrence. How about him?"

"We aren't Catholic Elliot. I'm Baptist and you're a Presbyterian. We'll get Theodore at the telegraph office to send out a wire."

"Maybe Theodore can marry us. He's got sense and education."

"He's not a minister."

"Who married everyone in the past?"

"Pastor, before he died."

"Oh."

"There are a few others around the county; some have even gone to some kind of seminary school up north I heard. So don't worry."

"I'm going to look into it, so I can conduct these ceremonies."

"That would be great Elliot. Make some money on the side."

I continued to preach at the church, with Naomi usually sitting in the front pew. She shined always, with colored sequined petticoats, high black leather boots, and black linen dresses and skirts.

Her hair was usually pinned up. I thought maybe she wanted to show off the sapphire gem stone clips that adorned each side of her head. But her face was one to shine -- absent her hair hanging down. Her high cheekbones, tanned face, sharp nose, smooth lips, and black eyebrows made her a sight to see. An open collared white shirt inside the petticoat accentuated her stature.

She was obviously proud of me, me being the preacher at church and writer at the newspaper. Ladies in the church would surround her with love and good tidings. They'd bring her gifts or food before service each Sunday. They would invite her to tea gatherings, picnics, and birthday parties. She was thriving as a result of her man being a preacher.

After church this Sunday, she said, as we were walking to her house, "We need a mid-week prayer meeting."

I looked at her blankly like I always do when I'm not sure about something.

"Why do we need that?"

"People need to be fed the word throughout the week. Several people are going through hard times, and it would give them something to look forward to."

"Well. That's understandable."

"You want to lead it?"

"No."

"Who can do it?"

"A layman of the church or a deacon. Anyone who knows the Bible and cares about people!"

"We don't have any layman. Got a couple deacons."

"They won't do it. One of them drinks occasionally and the other lives too far away."

"So that leaves me and you."

"It does."

"Elliot. I don't know how to lead a prayer meeting. Can you please help out? If I can get three people to come?"

"Whatever you want me to do Naomi, but remember, your father is sick and don't like to be bothered much right now."

"You're right. Let's consider it in the future, please?"

"Let's do."

She gave me one of those childish looks I would never be able to say no to.

"Sure," I said, figuring time was my ally in finding a person to lead a prayer meeting. Preaching I like, but listening to problems and giving advice is not one of my strong suits.

45.

We put a few other items in the newspaper.

Linda Tompkins was starting a tapestry shop, a young boy's puppy got run over by a wagon, and Gerard Davis's store sign blew down and caused buckboard damage to Willet Saproni's wagon.

We were now putting in a weather forecasting column, thanks to an almanac being passed around from a stranger who had arrived on a stagecoach.

And there was a small library being constructed, with funds from the railroad company leasing county land.

Wedding day was arriving fast, and I was feeling more comfortable by the hour. I had made the right choice, and from the looks of things, I'd be living with Naomi at her father's house.

When the first cold spell came, Jim's condition only worsened, and one morning, Naomi came hurriedly to the office and said, "Elliot. Daddy won't get up!"

"Maybe he's just over tired."

"No. It's been hours. He just lays there in bed with his mouth open.'

"I'll go right over."

"I'll go back with you."

I walked into his upstairs bedroom, and there he was, face up on the bed dead as a sack of cement. I touched him just to make sure, and his body was hard as a rock.

I walked back downstairs to where Naomi was nervously dusting off a table in the living room. "He's passed on Naomi."

Tears swelled in her eyes. "He said very little last night. Wouldn't eat a thing. What do we do now?"

"Call Brock Hastings the undertaker to come get him."

"And take him where?"

"He'll put him in a cool place until the burial."

"I'm glad he didn't suffer much. I tried to make it as easy on him as I could, but it was wearing on me."

"A person can only do so much for another person whose time it is to die. God is in charge of the affairs from death."

She came over, put her arms around me, and held on.

I caressed her and felt her sadness. I said, "The Lord gives and the Lord takes away. Jim will surely be rewarded with rest in heaven."

Naomi calmed herself and said "Yes. I better stay here today and think about this some, clean up, and get organized."

"Okay Naomi. I'll get Brock and Finklemeir."

205

I walked over to Finklemeir's office.

He was doctoring a man whose arm had got lassoed by a rope and burned, from what I heard in their conversation.

"Ain't nothing worse that a rope burn doc," the man said, as he held his arm out and Finklemeier was applying salve to it.

"Leave it on there. Should be alright in a couple days," the doctor said. "And wear a long sleeve shirt next time!"

The man walked out after laying a silver dollar on the table.

I spoke up and said, "Jim Morrisen died a little while ago. You and Brock mind coming over and taking care of the body."

"No. We will be there soon. Got two in the damper now staying cool, but we'll make room."

"Appreciate it."

I walked out the door and went back to Naomi's house

Naomi was cleaning up Jim's mess he had left: a half-eaten potato on a tin plate, a St. Louis Dispatch newspaper scattered on a nearby table, and wrinkled clothes that were lying beside him on the bed.

I told her Finklemeir would be over soon.

It wasn't long before Brock and Finklemeier came over and pushed the body onto a leather poled carrying bed.

Brock said they were taking it to the mortuary.

"To where?" I asked.

"A mortuary. We dug a hole in the ground a few feet deep where the earth is cool."

"Like a preserver."

"Yea. Lined it with talc and limestone to alkaline the air."

"So it will last a couple of days."

"At least. You conducting the funeral?"

"Ain't no one else to."

"Do within three days or there will be a problem."

I told Naomi to get one of Jim's suits. She ran to the closet, grabbed one, and gave it to Brock. Finklemeir was doing some kind of observation and temperature reading with an eyepiece and metal glass tube on Jim's arm.

I had used my hands to feel the cold pain of death saturating through Jim's lifeless form: no sense in making it complicated. I had done it on the battlefield many times.

Brock had the suit in his hands.

"Make him look good," I said.

Naomi got another suit out of the closet, came over to me, and said, "You'll look good in this one. Dad would want you to have it."

It was a black suit.

"Reckon you're right."

46.

The community had found out about the death by word of mouth, and in a couple days, we were all on Holy Hill behind the church with Jim in a pine box and me at the front of it. I was looking at the hole in the ground that had been dug, and his body alongside it on a couple of stands.

I had preached a few funerals after the Yankees had killed many of my comrades in the war. The hardest of them was when men had fallen short of crawling to the nearest mud puddle for a drink of water. There they lay, with a hand stretched out towards the water, head buried n the dirt -- as if trying to get moisture from the ground.

Many men were found with their heads lying to the north, as if God was waiting for them there, or maybe they were thinking the cool ice at the North Pole would make things better. Of course, Indians always sleep towards the north.

The easier funerals were for those who died on the spot. Some were sitting upright against a rock that had been protecting them. Others lay against a tree. No crawling for them.

I had looked at them and said goodbye. I thanked the Lord for their lives and hoped them to be spared from hell's torments.

The medics took care of the post mortem conditions: tallying up the final count of the dead, reporting them to the officers, and collecting valuables.

Since I knew the Bible well, I'd be called on to conduct services.

And then I'd go on my way to scouting duties.

When the war was over. I thought maybe that would be the end of that, but here I am a preacher, and my girlfriend's father has died. And there's not a preacher around who can get here within the time of preservation.

So I held my Bible in my hand in my new suit and started, "We are gathered here today to give honor and love to Jim Morrisen, who passed away three days ago in peace at home. He leaves behind his daughter, Naomi, and a cousin in Arizona. He came here with very little, got to know people, and started a newspaper, which brought people together. He was a fine pillar of the community. He has done his work, and may God say, 'Well done'. He loved the Lord and testified of his name; he was active in the church. The fourth Chapter, 10th verse of the Book of Hebrews says, for he that is entered into his rest, he hath ceased from his own works, as God has from his. May his soul rest in peace, and may we carry on the good works of the Lord."

I nodded for Brock to lower the body.

Naomi shed some tears and managed to throw fresh flowers on him, while Brock, Finklemeier, and Luke Garret lifted the box off its stands and put it into the ground.

As if their movements aggravated the clouds, or maybe it was God himself, a strong wind came along and nearly blew everyone's hats off.

I took it as a sign from God that he was in control of the situation and to take note of his presence.

47.

After the funeral, I walked Naomi home to be with her and get something to eat: a man can only live on corn pones for so long, and that's what I was normally cooking every night on the little stove at the office.

Jim's sister Hilda came with us, I suppose to make sure Jim's belongings and assets stayed in the family.

I didn't have any interest in them, but the suit coat and pants Naomi had given me fit great -- but garnered comments and stares from the church crowd.

"Hilda's going to Fred Bridgestone's smoke house to get a ham for dinner," Naomi said, when we got to the house.

"That would be great. Can I give you some money Hilda?"

"Wouldn't hurt. Fred does a lot of work keeping the fires going and smoking meat."

I gave Hilda a dollar, and she scampered off to Fred's farm just outside of town limits.

Naomi and I sat at the kitchen table staring into space. I suppose she was adapting to Jim being gone and me sitting in his seat. After a few minutes of silence, she said. "That was a nice funeral Elliot, the things you said about my father."

"Everyone deserves a good farewell on the final day."

"Except the wicked. What kind of farewell do they get?"

"Usually there's no farewell given."

Enough said, and Naomi had got me again.

We didn't have to speak, being comfortable with each other's presence and knowing the peace of God that passes all understanding. We did need to think about our marriage and its proper conduct. I wasn't sure what to say about it, but she took care of that for me.

" Theodore got word the preacher at Lawrence can't make it here until next month."

"Seems like a long time."

"Well. We need to do it right."

"A strange preacher don't make it right anyhow."

"Well. What can we do about it then?"

"I'm going to marry us once and for all."

She laughed a little and shook her head. "How you going to do that?"

"Give you my holy vow to protect, serve, and love you forever."

"I like it. I'll say one too."

"We need a witness."

"Don't a witness need to be a preacher?"

"No. A witness just looks and hears and signs the document."

"What kind of document?"

"A marriage document."

"That sounds good. Get Luke to go to the clerk's office and get one, and he can be our witness -- lay his hand on the Bible."

"I thought we were supposed to lay our hands on the Bible."

"No. You kiss me and give me a ring, not necessarily in that order, and we go have fun."

"Reckon what moon it is?"

"Whatever you want it to be. The full moon was a few days ago because the animals were fidgety and it was light out when I went out back in the middle of the night."

"I like the full moon. A man can see where he's walking at night and work some."

"Good for planting above the ground crops dad always said."

"What does Luke do?"

"Planting crops?"

"No. At the wedding."

"He listens to our vows and signs the document and registers it at town hall."

"That sounds good. Where's our honeymoon?"

"Right here cowboy."

"Aren't you supposed to throw something up in the air at the guests or something?"

"Yes. You got to get me some flowers."

"I can do that. Sounds like we're in love."

"You bet."

Naomi smiled and got up from the table to get some plates.

"Well, Don't just sit there Elliot. You're the man of the house now. The stove needs wood, Mercy and I need water, and mice keep coming in through the wall somewhere."

"I thought we were supposed to rest on Sunday."

"That's fine the when the house isn't falling apart and there are things to do."

"In that case, I'll get the wood, kill the mice, and feed the women."

"And can you please sharpen this knife," she said as she tried to cut through a potato. "It won't cut."

"You tried using the cutting edge?"

Naomi looked at it and saw the blade was upside down. Without a pause, she said, "Must have got turned around somehow."

I didn't respond to that, but it was so dull it was hard to tell what the sharp side was.

After I put some wood in the crate beside the stove, I went back outside and pumped some water into a bucket and pan for Naomi.

I brought them back inside. Shortly after, Hilda arrived with fresh pork loin chops and laid them on the counter.

"Fred butchered a hog yesterday -- said these were fresh as morning daisies."

The pieces had been cut in large triangles and were laced with white fat on the perimeters.

"They look good, pink enough. There's enough here for a couple days," Naomi said.

"Where do you store them?" I asked.

"Out back in the root cellar. There's a hole dug out to keep meats cool for a few days. Or we could salt them down for the winter, but Fred will have some smoked by then."

"We'll salt them down every couple of days to get the moisture out. Might want some for later.'

Naomi baked the loins and some sweet potatoes in the wood stove. She also boiled some cabbage leaves on top.

The dinner was good, Hilda went home, and I stayed for awhile and talked. We were both tired, not only from the funeral proceedings but from the cooking and housekeeping.

I told her to lock up well and I'd see her tomorrow – I was going to my bunk to study my marriage vows.

"You shouldn't have to study them Elliot. They're supposed to come from your heart."

"Well in that case, I'm ready. Let's move the date up since we know what we're doing."

"Maybe love is in the making."

"You think?"

"It's okay Elliot, but if you think moving the date up makes it better, let's do it."

"Jim's death has changed things."

"It did, and I would like you here."

"What about the moon?"

"The moon is always on the move."

"That settles it. We're getting married next week. People will still have time to get prepared."

"I hope I'm prepared," Naomi said.

"The Lord will prepare us."

48.

Naomi came to the office the next morning excited about something. Her face radiated with joy, a bounce was in her steps, and she was smiling.

"Good morning," I said.

"Hi. What a wonderful day!"

"What happened?"

"I felt so free this morning, I guess because I didn't have to wait on dad, cook, or clean up a mess!"

"He was becoming a burden, and it was showing on you."

"What are we doing today?"

"Need some stories, beside the periodic supplements, and I have to order supplies: ink, pencils, and paper. I've heard there are new presses available."

"That ordering book is on the top right shelf of dad's desk. You may as well sit there Elliot."

"Guess I could. Difficult to step in his place though."

"Why don't you move it farther towards the corner. Then it would be different."

"Good idea."

"One good place to get stories is from people who come by train or stage coach."

"Like personal interviews?"

"Something like that, but people want to read about what's going on outside of Kansas too."

"Okay. Maybe we need a gossip column.

"Sure Elliot. We can talk all about us."

I laughed. "Well, I forgot about that."

"I'll go to the livery stable and get a story about the latest breeds of horses available. People are always interested in that."

"Okay. I'll set the type for the latest events."

I woke up on my bunk the next morning and thought about several things.

I was getting used to working with Naomi on a full-time basis, but I was wondering how that was going to work when we'd be together all day and night after getting married.

The wedding preparations were keeping her happy: she was getting together with women and talking about the protocol, trying on dresses, and even promenading down the hallway several times at home.

I was talking with the local men about getting married. All of them said I had a real charm of a woman.

I was making new friends, and me being the new editor, made me more friends. Some people were clamoring for attention, others were politicking for special projects, and yet other wanted their opinions expressed about the state of affairs with the Indians, railroad, land grabs, and mineral rights.

Well, I knew all about that, and these interests by plain folk confirmed my feelings about being a part-time preacher, editor of the newspaper, and settling down with a woman like Naomi.

I thought about them vows for one minute, and then I decided thinking about them was only confusing matters. I'd say what I felt and hope it came out pleasing.

I had compared Naomi with other women, and she was always in first place: she worked hard, was compassionate, pretty, and she was a good cook. What more could a man ask for.

49.

Marriage day arrived with a swath of warm air over the
land, and I was thankful for it, because I wouldn't have to
wear my cowhide coat.

I got up slowly from my bunk and figured it to be the last
time I would sleep there. I sure hoped this marriage was going
to work. I was putting all my trust in God for it to work. It
seemed like Naomi didn't have a problem with getting
married – it was me calming down enough to settle down in
life and stay put.

I went to the creek to get a pot of water. I brought it back
inside, washed up, and put on Jim's suit.

Mr. Richards came over and escorted me to the church.
When we got there, he asked, "Who's going to marry you all?"

"God is going to marry us."

"Nothing better."

"Luke's going to witness our vows and register them with the clerk."

"That'll work."

Before I walked in the church, I grabbed some aster flowers and asked Mr. Richards to take them to Naomi.

He scampered off with them in his hand.

I went inside the church and sat on the front pew.

After a few minutes, people started filing in and sitting down. Walt closed the doors of the church, and it got quiet.

Luke came to the front, so I stood up and faced the crowd in Jim's black suit, all shaven and ready. I had purchased a gold ring from Stan Kinder, the local miner.

I waited and waited some more. The more I waited, the more doubtful I became about the wedding. I was aware of people shuffling in their seats, kids dropping marbles on the pew boards, and little girls giggling at whatever.

The doors opened, and in came Naomi surrounded by two women.

Luke looked at me like he was confused by the proceedings. He had never been married, so he wouldn't know what to do.

I thought to myself it wouldn't be quite right if I were conducting this ceremony, so I grabbed a Bible off the pew and gave it to Luke.

"Luke. It's not right I marry Naomi and I; so you will have to do it."

"I don't know what to do Elliot. I ain't never been married!"

"It's not difficult."

I held his gaze while turning to Book of Genesis. "All you do is read this little portion of words right here." And I pointed to where a man was to cleave to his wife.

He looked at it and said okay.

"Well, there is one more section that needs to be read."

I turned to Ephesians 5:22-31 and showed him that.

"I think I can do that," he said.

I dug into my suit pocket and handed him a ring.

"That for me?"

"No. You give it back to me and I'll put it on her finger after I give my vows. Then you say something like I can kiss the bride."

"Then it's over?"

"Almost. You got to say you pronounce Naomi and I man and wife as recognized by God and State of Kansas."

Naomi had come up to the altar and was just standing there smiling, with the flowers in her hand.

Her brass buttoned dark blue petticoat sparkled against her white collared shirt. It reminded me of Yankee garb and I thought to look for my rifle, but I came to my senses with her pretty black hair spread out among her shoulders and those white teeth showing through her smile.

She stepped a bit closer as if to say let's get on with it.

Luke stood back a little ways, while I stood like a stone statue.

She was smiling without a care in the world, while I was wondering what we would eat for lunch and who was going to make it. Maybe her girl friends had fixed it.

Luke got going pretty good: telling people why we were here, not to act up, and commemorate the day.

He even spoke our names out loud, and then he started reading what I had told him.

It came time for me to give my promise. I looked at Naomi and said, "Naomi Morrisen. I Elliot Grange, on this the 28th Day of September 1865, hereby promise to serve and love you the rest of my life. I promise to nurture you in all ways possible, to listen, pray, and help you in any way possible, for better, or for worse, and by the sovereign God who can help me. Amen."

She giggled a little and I wondered if I had messed up.

She turned her head to the crowd, as if looking for some affirmation she was doing the right thing; then she looked back at me.

"Elliot Grange. I Naomi Morrisen, duly swear and affirm to be a good wife and follow you all the days of my life."

And that was it.

The words made me shutter thinking of the responsibility, but surely, we'd be able to enjoy the good things in life.

Luke gave his spiel and gave me the ring, which I put on her finger.

She looked at the ring and at me in delight   then looked back at her friends and showed it off.

Women, I thought.

I nodded twice at Luke to tell me to kiss the bride.

Finally, he got the message when I put a finger to my mouth.

"You may kiss the bride!" he said.

So, I did.

She let go of the flowers and threw them into the air, grabbed mine, and led me out the front door to a wagon with a buckboard and horse.

It was a surprise to me, but I lifted Naomi up into it and jumped in and took the reins and headed the horse away.

"Where are we going Elliot?"

"Where would you like to go?"

I jerked the reins of the horse and stopped in front of Naomi's house.

"Wrong home," she said.

"Excuse me? And by the way, whose buckboard is this?"

"It's ours. The congregation got together and gave it as a gift."

"Lord be. How great is that?"

"Keep it going just outside of town."

I thought maybe Naomi wanted to go to the river and swim, but no, she stopped me in front of the ranch I had looked at outside of town that had a corral and corn shed.

"Right here," she said.

"This is a nice looking place – just needs a little work – patching the roof, cleaning the windows, and fixing the leaning columns on the porch."

"It's ours."

"Excuse me?"

"It is ours. Gordon Sanderson passed away and left it to the church – said he wanted a man of the word to have it."

"Holy jeez."

I got down off the wagon and stared at the old place, with its overgrown weeds, chipped boards where knots had fallen out, and tarred siding.

I looked back at Naomi, as she was still sitting on the wagon loosening the tight seam of the petticoat from around her neck.

"It's lovely," I said.

"There's one catch Elliot. The church is giving it to us on the condition you preach."

"Why certainly. I feel like I just arrived home!"

"You have Elliot. Dad left the other house to Aunt Hilda, knowing we'd have this one."

"Fair enough."

"Now can we go to the river?"

"You bet, Mrs. Grange."